He wanted Lindsey

And she needed him. She circled his neck with her arms, pulling him closer, deeper into the kiss. Her thighs brushed against his.

What he wouldn't give to carry her to bed and run his hands over every inch of her smooth skin. He stepped farther into the apartment, pulling her with him. Something crunched under his boot.

Bart drew back from the kiss and looked down. A smattering of letters and a mail-order catalog were strewn across the floor. A battered answering machine lay on the tile, its plastic casing in shards.

What was he thinking? Lindsey had been attacked here tonight. She could have been hurt. She could have been killed. She needed him, all right. But not to kiss her, not to make love to her. She needed him to keep her safe.

He looked up, peering into her intense blue eyes. "Pack your things."

"My things."

"You're moving out to the ranch. With me."

Dear Harlequin Intrigue Reader,

As you make travel plans for the summer, don't forget to pack along this month's exciting new Harlequin Intrigue books!

The notion of being able to rewrite history has always been fascinating, so be sure to check out *Secret Passage* by Amanda Stevens. In this wildly innovative third installment in QUANTUM MEN, supersoldier Zac Riley must complete a vital mission, but his long-lost love is on a crucial mission of her own! Opposites combust in *Wanted Woman* by B.J. Daniels, which pits a beautiful daredevil on the run against a fiercely protective deputy sheriff—the next book in CASCADES CONCEALED.

Julie Miller revisits THE TAYLOR CLAN when one of Kansas City's finest infiltrates a crime boss's compound and finds himself under the dangerous spell of an aristocratic beauty. Will he be the *Last Man Standing*? And in *Legally Binding* by Ann Voss Peterson—the second sizzling story in our female-driven in-line continuity SHOTGUN SALLYS—a reformed bad boy rancher needs the help of the best female legal eagle in Texas to clear him of murder!

Who can resist those COWBOY COPS? In our latest offering in our Western-themed promotion, Adrianne Lee tantalizes with *Denim Detective*. This gripping family-in-jeopardy tale has a small-town sheriff riding to the rescue, but he's about to learn one doozy of a secret.... And finally this month you are cordially invited to partake in *Her Royal Bodyguard* by Joyce Sullivan, an enchanting mystery about a commoner who discovers she's a betrothed princess and teams up with an enigmatic bodyguard who vows to protect her from evildoers.

Enjoy our fabulous lineup this month!

Sincerely,

Denise O'Sullivan
Senior Editor, Harlequin Intrigue

LEGALLY BINDING
ANN VOSS PETERSON

TORONTO • NEW YORK • LONDON
AMSTERDAM • PARIS • SYDNEY • HAMBURG
STOCKHOLM • ATHENS • TOKYO • MILAN • MADRID
PRAGUE • WARSAW • BUDAPEST • AUCKLAND

Special thanks and acknowledgment are given to
Ann Voss Peterson for her contribution
to the SHOTGUN SALLYS series.

ISBN 0-373-22780-9

LEGALLY BINDING

www.eHarlequin.com

Printed in U.S.A.

ABOUT THE AUTHOR

Ever since she was a little girl making her own books out of construction paper, Ann Voss Peterson wanted to write. So when it came time to choose a major at the University of Wisconsin, creative writing was her only choice. Of course, writing wasn't a *practical* choice—one needs to earn a living. So Ann found jobs ranging from proofreading legal transcripts to working with quarter horses to washing windows. But no matter how she earned her paycheck, she continued to write the type of stories that captured her heart and imagination—romantic suspense. Ann lives near Madison, Wisconsin, with her husband, her two young sons, her Border collie and her quarter horse mare. Ann loves to hear from readers. E-mail her at ann@annvosspeterson.com or visit her Web site at annvosspeterson.com.

Books by Ann Voss Peterson

HARLEQUIN INTRIGUE
579—INADMISSIBLE PASSION
618—HIS WITNESS, HER CHILD
647—ACCESSORY TO MARRIAGE
674—LAYING DOWN THE LAW
684—GYPSY MAGIC
     "Sabina"
702—CLAIMING HIS FAMILY*
723—INCRIMINATING PASSION
745—BOYS IN BLUE
     "Liam"
780—LEGALLY BINDING

*Top Secret Babies

All underlined places are fictitious.

CAST OF CHARACTERS

Lindsey Wellington—Eager to prove Bart Rawlins innocent, she jumps at the chance to defend him in court.

Bart Rawlins—After waking up with blood on his hands, a murder charge against him and no memory of the night before, Bart needs Lindsey to prove his innocence.

Jebediah Rawlins—When Bart's uncle winds up dead, and old family feud points to Bart as the prime suspect.

Hurley Zeller—What kind of grudge does the deputy have against Bart?

Gary Tuttle—Does the foreman at the Four Aces Ranch know more than he's letting on?

Kenny Rawlins—Could Bart's cousin have killed his own father for his inheritance?

Brandy Carmichael—Who is the mystery blonde?

Paul Lambert—Lindsey's boss has faith in her. Is it well-founded?

Donald Church—The wills and trusts attorney may know all the Rawlins family secrets, but he's keeping them to himself.

Nancy Wilks—Does the office administrator of Lambert & Church know more than she should about the firm's clients?

Beatrice Jensen—The geriatric nurse has a secret of her own.

Shotgun Sally—The legendary frontierswoman influences the lives of Kelly, Lindsey and Cara in their quest for the truth!

To Denise O'Sullivan, Lynda Curnyn and Allison Lyons.
Thanks for inviting me to Mustang Valley.

To Susan Kearney and Linda O. Johnston.
Thanks for exploring Mustang Valley with me.

And a special thanks to Jack, Sandy, Kevin and Troy Jones
for introducing me to the state of Texas
all those years ago!

Chapter One

Bart Rawlins forced one eye open. Late-morning sun slanted through his bedroom window, blinding him. Pain, sharper than his old Buck knife, drilled into his skull. He gripped the edge of the mattress and willed the room to stop spinning.

He hadn't had that much to drink at Wade Lansing's Hit 'Em Again Saloon last night, had he? Not enough to warrant a hangover like this.

He remembered hitching a ride to the bar with Gary Tuttle, his foreman at the Four Aces Ranch. Remembered wolfing down some of Wade's famous chili and throwing back a few beers. Not enough to make his head feel like it was about to explode. Not enough to make his mouth taste like an animal had crawled in and died.

Damn, but he was too old for this. At thirty-five, he always thought he would be settled down with a woman he loved, raising sons and daughters to take over the Four Aces Ranch. Instead he was lying in bed with his boots on and a hangover powerful enough to split his skull.

He raised a hand to his forehead. His fingers felt sticky on his skin. Sticky and moist and smelled like—

His eyes flew open and he jerked up off the mattress. Head throbbing, he stared at his splayed fingers. Something brown coated his hands and had settled into the creases of work-worn skin. The same rusty-brown flecked his Wranglers.

Blood.

What the hell? Had he gotten drunk and picked a fight? Was a well-aimed punch responsible for his throbbing head?

Bart pushed himself off the bed and stumbled to the bathroom. Peering into the mirror, he checked his face. Although his nose was slightly crooked from a fall off a horse when he was ten, it looked fine. So did the rest of his face. And a quick check of other body parts turned up nothing, either. The blood must have come from the other guy.

The doorbell's chime echoed through the house.

Who the hell could that be? He tried to scan his memory for an appointment this morning, but his sluggish mind balked.

The doorbell rang again. Whoever it was, he wasn't going away.

Bart turned on the water and plunged his hands into the warm stream. He splashed his face, grabbed a towel and headed down the stairs. He'd better answer the door before the bell woke his dad. Good thing the old man was a heavy sleeper. Bart would get rid of whoever it was so he could nurse his hangover in peace. And try to remember what in the hell had happened last night.

He reached the door and yanked it open.

As wide as he was tall, Deputy Hurley Zeller looked up at Bart through narrowed little eyes. The sheriff's right-hand man had a way of staring that made a man feel he'd done something illegal even if he hadn't. And ever since Bart beat him out as starting quarterback in high school, he'd always saved his best accusing stare for Bart.

Bart shifted his boots on the wood floor. "What's up, Hurley?"

"I have bad news."

Bart rooted his boots to the spot. If he'd learned one thing about bad news in his thirty-five years, it was that it was best to take it like a shot of rotgut whiskey. Straight up and all at once. "What is it?"

"Your uncle Jebediah. He's dead."

Bart blew a stream of air through tight lips. Uncle Jeb's death meant there would be no reconciliation. No forgiveness to mend the feud in the Rawlins clan that had started the day Bart's granddad died and left his son Hiriam a larger chunk of the seventy-thousand-acre ranch. Now it was too late for a happy ending to that story. "Well, that is bad news, Hurley. Real bad. How did he die?"

Hurley focused on the leather pouch on Bart's belt, the pouch where he kept his Buck knife. "Maybe I should ask you that question."

Bart draped the towel over one shoulder and moved his hand to the pouch. It was empty. The folding hunting knife he'd hung on his belt since his father gave it to him for his fourteenth birthday was gone. Shock jolted Bart to the soles of his Tony Lamas. "You don't think I killed—" The question lodged in his throat. He followed Hurley's pointed stare to the towel on his shoulder.

The white terry cloth was pink with blood.

A smile spread over Hurley's thin lips. "I think you're coming with me, Bart. And you've got the right to remain silent."

LINDSEY WELLINGTON ADJUSTED her navy-blue suit, tucked her Italian leather briefcase under one arm and marched toward the Mustang County jail and her first solo case. She hadn't been this nervous since she'd taken the Texas bar exam. At least her years at Harvard Law School had given her plenty of experience taking tests. This was a different story. This was real life.

This was murder.

She'd explained to Paul Lambert and Donald Church, senior partners of Lambert & Church, that she hadn't specialized in criminal law. She'd also reminded them she didn't have trial experience, that either of them would be far more qualified. But they'd insisted she take the case anyway. Even though both Paul and Don had backgrounds that included criminal law, Lambert & Church didn't have a true criminal attorney on staff. Not since Andrew McGovern had died in the annex fire last month. Not since Andrew was *murdered,* she corrected herself. A murder that wouldn't have been discovered, let alone solved, if not for her dear friend, Andrew's sister Kelly, and Kelly's new husband Wade Lansing.

Lindsey pushed into the air-conditioned lobby of the jail, checked in at the desk and followed a deputy back to a small visiting room to wait for her client.

Her client.

A shiver crept up her spine at the thought. She tried to quell it. She couldn't afford to be nervous. This case was the opportunity she'd been waiting for. Over fifteen hundred miles from her well-meaning family's influence and penchant for pulling strings to help her, she was finally getting a chance to prove herself on her own terms.

She set her briefcase on the table and took a calming breath. She couldn't let her client know how nervous she was. Or how little experience she had. If she wanted to prove herself a professional, she had to act like one.

The door swung wide and a deputy led a tall man wearing an orange jumpsuit into the room. Lindsey looked up into a tanned face and sparkling green eyes, and struggled to catch her breath. It was a good thing she was sitting because her knees felt weak.

When she'd imagined defending an alleged murderer named Bart Rawlins, she'd pictured Black Bart, the infamous outlaw. Big and mean, with coal black hair to match his black hat. But the man who folded his big frame into the chair opposite her couldn't be further from that image. With the body of Adonis and blond visage to match, he looked more like a hero straight from the silver screen.

"You must be Lindsey Wellington." He held out a hand. "I'm Bart Rawlins."

She shook his hand, a thrill skittering over her skin at the touch of work-roughened fingers. "Don't worry, Mr. Rawlins. I'll get you out of here immediately." Her voice sounded breathless in her ear. As breathless as she felt. She inwardly cringed.

"Call me Bart. Paul and Don said you were the best criminal lawyer in the firm."

The best? So they hadn't told him they'd handed his case to a lawyer who'd just passed the bar. "Paul and Don exaggerate. But I'll *do* my best, Bart. I promise you that."

"I'm sure you will." He tilted his head to study her, the fluorescent lights overhead gleaming off his sun-bleached hair. "They forgot to tell me you were the prettiest lawyer in the firm, too. Hell, I'd be willing to bet you're the prettiest lawyer in the whole damn county."

To Lindsey's horror, a warm flush inched up her neck and burned her cheeks. "I—we should—I mean, thank you," she finished lamely. What was wrong with her? She was blushing and stammering like a teenager with a crush.

"So where do we start?" he asked.

She looked at Bart, her mind a blank.

"My defense. Where should we start?"

She snatched herself out of the idiot-trance that had grabbed her the moment he'd strode into the room.

She had to pull herself together. She was a professional. "Tell me what happened last night."

He ran a big hand over his face and shook his head as if he'd already told the story more times than he cared to remember. "I went to Wade Lansing's place, a saloon down on Main Street called Hit 'Em Again. I shot some pool, downed a few beers and found myself at home with a hangover to wake the dead."

"What time did you leave the bar?"

"That's the problem. I don't remember."

"You don't remember the time?"

He grimaced. "I don't remember leaving."

She tried to keep her surprise from showing on her face. Bart Rawlins didn't strike her as a heavy drinker. In the high-pressure world of law in which her family lived, heavy drinkers abounded. But all the heavy drinkers she'd known in her twenty-six years had an air of despair about them that was lacking in Bart. "How many beers did you drink?"

"Three. Four, tops."

She looked him up and down, trying to ignore the tightening sensation low in her stomach at the sight of his long, lean legs and broad muscled shoulders. With his size, three or four beers shouldn't lead to a blackout. But then, people often underestimated their alcohol consumption. "Are you sure you didn't have more?"

"To tell the truth, the whole night is kind of fuzzy. But I usually only drink three or four. Maybe I did have more."

"How did you get home?"

He shook his head, obviously at a loss for an answer.

"You didn't drive, did you?"

"I didn't have my truck. I hitched a ride to the tavern with my ranch foreman. Maybe I left with him. I don't remember."

"I'll talk to him. And a talk with the bartender might shed some light on exactly how much you drank." Lindsey jotted notes on her legal pad. "Of course there's always the possibility that you were drugged."

His eyebrows shot up. "Drugged?"

"Rohypnol or something similar. The date-rape drug."

"Date-rape drug?"

"It's an illegal tranquilizer that causes blackouts."

"I've heard of it in the news. But who would give me something like that?"

"Someone who wanted to make sure you took the fall for your uncle's murder."

He nodded, a frown claiming his brow. "Then what about the blood? Where did that come from?"

She clamped her bottom lip between her teeth. "What blood?"

"When I woke up, I had blood all over my hands and clothes. At first I thought I must have gotten in a brawl. But I don't have any scrapes or bruises."

"Did the deputies take samples of the blood?"

"Sure did. A load of pictures, too."

The start of a headache pulsed behind her eyes. If the prosecution tied the blood on Bart's hands and clothes to his uncle by DNA tests, Bart was as good as convicted. Only O.J. had beaten evidence like that. And he hadn't been tried in Texas.

"There's another thing."

She almost flinched. "What?"

"My knife. A Buck Model One-Ten. It's missing. And from the look on Hurley Zeller's face when he arrested me, he knows where it is."

"At the murder scene."

"That's my guess." His voice was heavy, as if his charm and good humor had finally given way under the weight of the evidence against him. Or maybe he'd just read her face.

She forced a confident smile. "We'll find the answers. Don't worry."

He nodded, but judging from the pallor under his tan, he wasn't buying her strained optimism.

"The first thing we have to do is get you out of here. Do you have money or property to put up for bail? It'll be pretty high."

He waved a hand. "I can come up with the money."

She nodded, grateful for a development that was positive, even if it was merely a matter of available cash. "I'll push for a bail hearing. Then we need to get you to a doctor as soon as possible to test for drugs. If we can prove you were drugged, at least we'll have something to fight with."

"I didn't kill him, Ms. Wellington."

The naked honesty aching in his voice brought tears

to her eyes. She blinked them back. "You don't have to tell me that, Bart."

"I want to. No matter what differences I or my father had with my uncle, I didn't kill him. I wouldn't kill anyone."

"Your father?"

Bart's eyes narrowed. "My daddy is sick. Even if he wasn't, he'd never kill his own brother any more than I would kill my uncle."

"Of course." Lindsey nodded. "We just have to prove it. And we will."

"Am I looking at the death penalty?"

"No. They'll charge you with first-degree murder. Only capital murder carries the death penalty in Texas, and for this case to be classified as capital murder, there would have to be other factors involved."

"Other factors?"

"Like the victim was a police officer. Or the murder was intentionally committed in the course of another felony. Or more than one person was killed as part of the same scheme or course of conduct. The most severe sentence you can get for a first-degree murder charge is life in prison."

"That sounds the same as death to me." Elbows on the table, he tented his fingers in front of his mouth and blew a stream of air through them. "Give it to me straight. My chances don't look good, do they?"

If she had more experience, maybe she would have been ready for the question. She'd have a prepared spiel that was both comforting and realistic. As it was, she didn't have a clue what to say.

''That bad, huh?''

''No. Not that bad. We'll get to the truth, Bart. I promise.''

He dropped his arms to his sides and looked deeply into her eyes. ''Thank you, Ms. Wellington.''

''You can call me Lindsey.''

''Thank you, Lindsey.''

A shiver crept up her spine at the sound of his Texas drawl caressing her name. But this time the shiver wasn't only the result of physical attraction, it was one of fear. Because this time, losing didn't mean embarrassing herself in moot court or lowering her grade point average.

This time losing could cost a man his freedom.

Chapter Two

Bart grimaced as the needle sank into the tender spot at the inside of his elbow. Once the needle was in place, Doc Swenson attached the vacuum tube, filling the vial with deep red blood. His blood. Blood that, if he was lucky, might still be spiked with Rohypnol or some other drug. "Damn."

Lindsey Wellington leaned her sweet body close. The scent of roses tickled his nose. Her shiny chestnut hair draped over one shoulder and brushed his arm despite the clips securing it back from her face. "Does it hurt?"

"What, the possibility of being a victim of the date-rape drug? Damn straight it hurts. It hurts my sense of manhood."

A smile teased the corners of her soft-looking lips. "I doubt your sense of manhood is that fragile."

"Maybe not when you're around. You're ladylike enough to make even a gelding feel like a stud."

That pretty pink color stained her cheeks again. God, she was a beautiful woman, delicate as a China doll with her clear blue eyes, porcelain skin and long, silky hair. But that wasn't all. In addition to looks, Lindsey Wellington had intelligence to burn and a refined Boston accent that reminded him of the Kennedy family.

And she was his lawyer. Amazing.

With the possible exception of Paul Lambert and Don Church, he'd grown up with a healthy belief that lawyers were bloodsuckers at best, sharks at worst. But Lindsey Wellington had destroyed every preconceived notion in his head the moment he laid eyes on her.

It was a damn shame he hadn't met her last week, last month. Before he had a murder charge hanging over his head. Maybe he wouldn't have been at Hit 'Em Again last night. Maybe he would have been too busy trying to win her to be hanging out at the local watering hole. It was a twist of fate too cruel to be believed that he'd finally found a woman who set a spur in his side when he couldn't do a damn thing about it.

Doc Swenson pulled the filled vial from the needle in his arm, capped it and attached an empty one in its place. More blood flowed.

"Are you planning to drain me dry, Doc?"

The crusty old coot peered at him over little reading glasses. "Word has it you're the one draining people dry, Bart. The whole town is talking about what you did to your uncle Jeb."

He should have known. He'd been arrested just this morning, but waiting for a bail hearing had taken much of the day. He shouldn't be surprised that the news of his arrest for murdering Jeb had already swept through town. Gossip traveled fast in Mustang Valley. Especially gossip over something as juicy as family feuds and murder. Of course Doc would have learned about Jeb's murder even without the gossip. Jeb's body was probably waiting in the autopsy room this very minute for Mustang Valley's only doctor and coroner to poke and prod. "I didn't kill Jeb, Doc."

Doc waved a hand, as if he hadn't believed it from the beginning. But the sharpness in his old blue eyes suggested different. He nodded at Bart's arm. "What do you want this blood for, anyway?"

"We want to have it tested for any kind of drug that might have altered Bart's consciousness. We also need a urinalysis done for Rohypnol or any similar tranquilizer," Lindsey explained.

Doc capped the second vial, pulled out the needle and snapped off the rubber tourniquet wrapping Bart's biceps. Rummaging through stacks of supplies on the adjacent counter, he grabbed a plastic specimen cup. He held it out to Bart. "Fill this."

Bart looked down at the cup and shifted his boots on the floor. Discussing bodily functions had never bothered him before. He was a cowboy born and bred, used to dealing with anything cattle or horses could come up with. But somehow with Lindsey looking on, his bodily functions took on an entirely different meaning. And focus. He forced himself to take the cup from Doc's hand.

"So you think he got drugged up the night of Jeb's

murder?'' Doc smiled stiffly at Lindsey, the old buzzard's best shot at charm.

Lindsey ignored the doc's question. "When can you have the results?"

Doc's smile faded. "We don't have a lab here. Got to send the sample out."

Lindsey nodded and fished a card from her briefcase. She scrawled something on the back and handed it to the doc. "Here's the lab I'd like it sent to. And on the back, I've written my home address. Have them send the results there and to my office. I want to make sure I see them as soon as they come in."

Doc took the card. "Could take a few days, could take a few months, depending on how busy the lab is. Then there's always the chance the drug won't show up at all."

"What do you mean? If it's in his system, it should show up, right?"

Doc scowled down at Bart. "Boy, what time did you take those drugs last night?"

"I didn't take drugs, Doc."

"Well, what the hell is this good-looking lady asking me about then?"

"Someone might have put something in my beer last night when I wasn't paying attention. A drug to make me black out."

"More likely you just got a little too friendly with a whiskey bottle."

Bart expelled a frustrated breath.

"What were you saying about the drugs not showing up in Bart's system?" Lindsey asked.

The old man turned his attention back to Lindsey. "If too much time has passed since Bart took those drugs, they won't show up on the screens."

Lindsey worried her bottom lip between straight white teeth. "I thought it took twenty-four hours for the drug to clear."

"That's right. But Bart's a big boy, so it might take a lot less."

A weight descended on Bart's chest. The clock on the wall of Doc's little examination room read six o'clock. Twenty-one hours had already passed since his last memory of the saloon. If Doc was right about his size making the time shorter, they were cutting it close. Damn close.

He glanced at Lindsey and closed his fingers tighter around the plastic cup. "I'll be right back."

She nodded. Judging from the worry creases digging into that pretty forehead, she'd noticed the time as well. If the substance was no longer in his system, he couldn't prove he was drugged. And if he couldn't prove his amnesia was real, he wouldn't have much of a defense, no matter how pretty and smart his lawyer was.

BART HELD THE DOOR of the Hit 'Em Again Saloon for Lindsey and followed her inside. The place was nearly empty except for a couple of regulars at the pool table, the cowboys and working men who filled the place nightly still hard at work this early in the evening. On the jukebox, Dale Watson belted out a real country song, the music echoing off the empty postage-stamp dance floor.

They crossed to the oak bar and bellied up. The smell of stale cigarette smoke warred with the bleach-like smell of bar sanitizer, but it was the soft scent of roses that held Bart's attention. He leaned closer to Lindsey and took a deep breath.

"You don't usually drink beer this early, Bart. Need a little hair of the dog that bit you?" Wade Lansing pushed through the swinging door leading back to the kitchen and took his usual spot behind the bar. Despite his flip statement, Bart could see the worry lining his friend's face. Worry focused on him.

Bart glanced at Lindsey. "Lindsey, this is Wade Lansing, the owner of this fine establishment."

"You mean beer joint," Wade said.

"Beer joint with the best food west of the Mississippi," Bart threw in.

Wade grinned. "Nice to see you again, Lindsey." Wade cleared a couple of highball glasses from the bar, the gold band on his finger shining in the bar's dim light.

"I thought you and Kelly were supposed to be on your honeymoon by now," Bart said.

"I'm training a kid to take over this place while I'm gone. Don't want to come back to find the till empty and the building burned to the ground."

Lindsey nodded. "Kelly said the two of you are planning to go to Hawaii. Sounds wonderful."

"We could go anywhere as far as I'm concerned. As long as Kelly is with me, I'm happy. I'm glad to hear you're representing Bart here, Lindsey. It'll keep me from worrying." He zeroed in on Bart. The grin turning his lips faded. "The whole town is talking about you."

"I didn't kill Jeb, Wade."

"I know that. But Hurley Zeller doesn't share my opinion. He was in here as soon as I opened, asking questions."

"Damn." Bart grimaced. Hurley sure had a leg up on them. Bart still didn't have a clue what had happened. He hoped Wade could give them some answers.

Lindsey set her briefcase on the bar, opened it and pulled out a pad of paper and pen. "We'd appreciate anything you can tell us about last night, Wade."

"Like what you told Hurley," Bart said.

"I didn't tell that prick anything."

Bart couldn't keep the grin off his face. Wade might be happily married, but he still hadn't shed his distrust for authority.

"What do you remember seeing?" Lindsey asked.

"I set up a few bottles of beer and served Bart up some chili. Then I had to duck out to change some big bills." Wade grabbed a dirty glass and plunged it up and down on a dishwashing contraption made of spinning brushes located in a sink behind the bar. "When I got back, you were fall-down drunk, Bart. I figured you must have been doing some serious whiskey-drinking while I was gone. Though I've never known you to drink more than a few beers."

Bart and Lindsey exchanged looks. Wade's description jibed with their theory that Bart was drugged. Unfortunately, it could also be a description of a man who'd simply sucked down too much whiskey.

"Who served drinks while you were gone?" Lindsey asked.

"The kid I'm training to fill in for me." Wade jotted something on a cocktail napkin and handed it to Lindsey before resuming glass-washing. "That's his name and number. He has tonight off, but otherwise you can also find him here."

"Thanks." Lindsey stowed the napkin in her briefcase. "When did Bart leave and who did he leave with?"

Wade stopped the plunging motion and glanced up at Bart. "Blackout?"

Bart nodded.

Wade looked at Lindsey. "The place was hopping last night, but best I can remember, he left around midnight. I just assumed he rode back to the ranch with his foreman, Gary Tuttle, same way he came. I can ask around tonight, see if anyone saw different." Wade dipped the glass in the sink full of sanitizer and set in on a mat to drip-dry. "Are you going to tell me what was going on last night, Bart? You aren't one to drink till you black out."

"We think Bart was drugged," Lindsey supplied. "Maybe Rohypnol or something similar."

Wade didn't look surprised. "There's something strange going on in Mustang Valley. First Andrew and now this."

Bart couldn't agree more. The revelation that Andrew McGovern had been murdered by Mustang Valley's mayor had been a shock. And now Jeb. Two murders in two months. Not to mention the mayor's fatal car accident. "The problem is, I don't know if I can prove I was drugged. Hurley might have kept me tied up in jail too long for the tests to show the drug in my system."

"What if you could find the bottles you were drinking out of?"

Lindsey leaned toward Wade. "You said the bar was busy last night. There must be hundreds of bottles. Can you really find the ones Bart drank out of?"

"My friend here has an annoying habit of peeling the label off every bottle of beer he drinks." He glanced at his watch. "This place will be full of cowboys soon, so I don't have time to look. But if you want to sort through the bottle bins out back, be my guest."

"It's worth a shot." Lindsey looked to Bart. "Do you want to help me search through empty beer bottles?"

"I'll sort through a thousand bottles if it will help prove I didn't kill Jeb."

"Then let's get started."

They slid off their bar stools and followed Wade through the prep kitchen and out Hit 'Em Again's back door. Wade pointed toward a Dumpster in the narrow alley. On one side of it was a row of large trash cans. Wade nodded toward them. "Have at it." Turning, he ducked back into the bar.

Bart glanced at Lindsey's sharply pressed suit, gossamer stockings and polished nails. "I'll do the searching."

Lindsey set her briefcase on the ground and pushed up her sleeves. "It'll go a lot faster if we both search."

He held up a hand. "I insist. A lady like you shouldn't be rummaging around in garbage."

Lindsey flashed him a pointed grin. "You forget. I'm no lady, I'm a lawyer."

Bart couldn't keep a laugh from bubbling out. "All right, then. But as far as I'm concerned, you're a lady. A real smart one."

She looked away from him before he could see if she was blushing again and set to work picking through the brown-glass bottles.

Suddenly footsteps and voices rose above the clank of glass hitting glass. Bart turned just in time to see his cousin Kenny round the building and stride into the alley, his black felt Stetson slung low over his eyes. "I heard you were here. I should have known you'd be hiding in a back alley," Kenny slurred, his voice rough with cigarettes and soggy with booze.

Bart hadn't spoken to Uncle Jeb's son in years. And he sure didn't want to start tonight. But it looked like he had no choice. "What do you want?"

"I want to know why the hell you aren't in jail."

"I don't want trouble, Kenny."

"You can take a knife to an old drunk's throat, but when it comes to fighting an able man, you don't want trouble?"

A good-looking blonde walked into the alley and stopped a few steps behind Kenny. Frowning, she folded her arms across her ample chest, like she was turned off by the prospect of her boyfriend picking a fight. A smattering of other spectators who'd apparently followed Kenny's bluster hung back in the shadows, content to watch from a distance.

Bart glanced at Lindsey. She watched Kenny the way a person eyed a car crash, repulsed but unable to look away. Bart shook his head. He didn't want to get into a family brawl in front of her. Hell, he didn't want her to know Kenny was family at all.

He pulled his gaze from Lindsey and focused on his cousin. Kenny had been an ornery cuss since the day he was born. But he'd also just lost his father—a father he despised, but his father, nonetheless. It was probably natural he'd want to blame Bart. Especially when the law was blaming Bart, too. "Listen, Kenny. I didn't kill Jeb."

"And you expect me to believe you?"

"I'm telling God's honest truth."

"The same truth your daddy told when he talked Grandad into leaving him most of the Four Aces Ranch?"

Bart almost groaned. It was still about the ranch. "When Grandad died, Jeb didn't want any part of working the ranch. He never did. He just didn't want my daddy to have it. Look what he's done with the land Grandad gave him. Nothing."

"He didn't have it as easy as your daddy."

"And why was that? Because he liked to drink more than he liked to work?" Bart tried to bite back the words, but it was too late. He'd had it with Kenny's whining and excuses for his good-for-nothing daddy and himself.

Kenny balled his hands into fists and swaggered closer. "Maybe Jeb was a bastard and a drunk. Maybe he deserved what he got. But that doesn't mean I shouldn't get my fair share. Or are you planning to kill me too and take it all?"

Bart held up his hands, palms facing Kenny. "I didn't kill Jeb, Kenny. And that's all I'm going to say about it."

Kenny stepped closer. The stench of cheap whiskey wafted on his breath. He jabbed a fist at Bart. The punch missed. "Gonna pull out your knife, Bart? Oh, that's right. The police confiscated it after you used it to kill your own flesh and blood."

Lindsey stepped forward. "How do you know about Bart's knife?"

Kenny didn't bother to give her a glance, as if she wasn't important enough to answer.

Bart tried to keep a lid on his simmering temper. Getting into a fistfight with Kenny wouldn't do anyone any good. "Go home and sleep it off, Kenny."

"Won't change anything. When I wake up, my old man will still be dead, and you'll still be the one to blame." He threw another punch. His fist plowed into Bart's arm, connecting solidly this time.

Bart's arm throbbed with the blow. His own hands clenched into fists. Grieving or not, one more hit and Kenny was history. "I wouldn't do that again if I were you."

"Or what? You going to sic your whore on me?" He leered at Lindsey and drew back his arm.

Bart didn't wait for Kenny's next punch to fall. His own fist was already flying.

Chapter Three

Lindsey stared in horror as Bart's big fist plowed into Kenny's middle.

Kenny hunched over and stumbled to the side. He slammed into a bottle bin and fell. The receptacle tipped over. Glass shattered. Bottles scattered along the ground, brown glass everywhere.

The blonde who'd entered the alley with Kenny ran to his side. "Kenny? Are you all right?"

Kenny sputtered, as if trying to catch his breath. "You saw that. He attacked me. He tried to kill me."

Bart loomed over him. "If I'd tried to kill you, you'd be dead. Now get the hell out of here."

The blonde grabbed Kenny's arm, pulling him to his feet and toward the mouth of the alley. "You heard him, Kenny. Let's go."

Kenny shrugged off her hold. "I ain't going nowhere. He tried to kill me. You saw it. I want the sheriff. Somebody call the sheriff. I want to press charges."

Lindsey almost groaned. The last thing Bart needed was for the sheriff's department to get involved. The court could decide to revoke his bail over this. He'd be locked in jail awaiting trial. "You threw the first punch, Mr. Rawlins. I think you'll be hard-pressed to prove Bart tried to kill you."

Kenny's mouth flattened into a hard line. His eyes narrowed. "What do you know about it?"

"Plenty." She fished a card from the pocket of her suit jacket and thrust it at him, hoping her profession would give him pause. "I'm a lawyer."

He squinted at the card, then looked up at Bart. "So she's not your whore after all. She's worse. She's your goddamn lawyer."

Bart charged Kenny.

Spinning on his heel, Kenny scampered from the alley. Once he was a safe distance away, he looked over his shoulder. "I'll get you, Bart. You won't get away with what you've done."

The door of the tavern flew open and Wade Lansing stepped out. Assessing the situation through narrowed gray eyes, he walked over to Bart. "What the hell is going on out here?"

While Bart explained what had happened, Lindsey watched the small crowd that had followed Kenny to the alley disperse. A single woman stayed and stepped out from the shadows, the light from the setting sun turning her curls to fire. She scribbled notes on a pad of paper.

Cara.

Under normal circumstances, Lindsey would be happy to see one of the few good friends she'd made since moving to Mustang Valley. But these circumstances were anything but normal. Cara Hamilton was a reporter for the *Mustang Gazette.* And next to the sheriff or one of his deputies, a reporter was the last person Lindsey wanted to see right now. Even if it was Cara.

She darted around Wade and Bart. She couldn't do anything to change what had happened between Bart and Kenny, but maybe she could appeal to Cara not to splash the news all over Mustang Valley. "Hey, Cara."

Cara brushed a curl from her forehead and looked up from her notebook. "Hi, Lindsey. How are you mixed up in this? Are you representing Bart Rawlins?" Cara's eyes flashed with inquisitiveness, her pen poised over paper.

Great. Lindsey hadn't taken into account that *she* might be part of Cara's story. "Are you covering Jeb Rawlins's murder?"

"Of course not." Cara rolled her eyes. "Beau is keeping the good stories to himself as usual."

Lindsey nodded. Cara's editor, and owner of the *Mustang Gazette,* Beau Jennings, had covered every major story in Mustang Valley for the past forty-some years. "He knows once he gives you a major story, the Dallas papers will snatch you up in a heartbeat."

Cara tilted her head. "Of course, having a friend representing Bart Rawlins might just give me the break I need. So are you Bart's lawyer, Lindsey?" she asked again.

Lindsey should have known changing the subject wouldn't throw Cara off. Once her friend smelled a story, she didn't give up until she rooted out the truth.

Lindsey sighed. "Yes."

"Why the heavy sigh? Is his case that bad?"

"No."

"He has a strong case then?"

She gave her friend a warning smile. "Quit fishing, Cara."

"Then talk to me."

"Off the record?"

"Okay."

"Don't print anything about this ridiculous fight."

"You're kidding, right? This is news, Lindsey. I can't just pretend I didn't see what happened."

She let out another sigh. "No, I suppose you can't. I'm just worried about poisoning the jury pool."

"I don't know what it's like in a big city like Boston, but gossip travels like dust in a strong wind around here. Even if I don't write about what happened, people will hear about it. And there's no telling what kind of twisted version they'll get."

"I suppose you're right."

"Damn straight." Cara's hazel eyes twinkled with humor.

Lindsey tried to return her smile, but her attempt fell flat.

"But you don't have to worry. I'll tell the whole story."

She gave Cara a questioning look.

"Meaning, I'll be writing that Kenny came looking for Bart and threw the first punch. I'll also include a bit of background, like Kenny's conviction for fraud."

"He's been convicted?"

"Kenny Rawlins is a master of the get-rich-quick scam. He's cheated a lot of people in Mustang Valley, a fact my readers won't easily forget."

Lindsey pressed her lips into a line. It wasn't a great situation, but she could live with it. "Thanks, Cara."

"For what? Telling the truth?" Cara smiled. "If you really want to thank me, give me a few quotes about Bart's case."

Lindsey took a deep breath of evening air. She supposed it was only fair she give her friend a quote. "He's an innocent man. You can print that. And I'll give you the scoop on who's guilty as soon as I find out."

BART WATCHED a single set of approaching headlights play across Lindsey's flawless skin. His attention trailed to her long, elegant fingers wrapped around the steering wheel of her little white sports car. On her right hand, a platinum ring with some kind of red stone glowed in the dashboard light. Her left ring finger was free of jewelry.

He tried to concentrate on the ribbon of highway stretching from Mustang Valley to the Four Aces Ranch. He shouldn't be noticing Lindsey's skin and fingers and whether she was wearing a wedding ring. She was his lawyer, not a pretty young thing he'd met at some honky-tonk.

Besides, he had more pressing things to deal with than a crush he couldn't do anything about. Like being accused of murdering his uncle. Like the real possibility he would be spending the rest of his life behind bars. Even if Lindsey wasn't his lawyer and far out of his league, he couldn't do a damn thing about his attraction to her. Not with the prospect of spending the rest of his life in Huntsville hanging over his head.

After Kenny had left the alley, he and Lindsey had resumed their search for beer bottles with missing labels. All they'd come up with were two bottles and a few shards of glass from the bin Kenny had tipped over. Tomorrow morning Lindsey planned to drive to Fort Worth to drop off the bottles and shards at the same lab where Doc had sent the other samples. A long shot, but better than nothing.

Of course, if it hadn't been for Lindsey's theory about the drug, he wouldn't have a shot at all.

His focus drifted back to her face. Her eyebrows knit together. She gnawed on her lower lip. All in all, she looked as worried as he felt. "What are you thinking about?" he asked.

She started at his voice, then glanced at him briefly before bringing her attention back to the road ahead. "Your cousin, Kenny. Cara Hamilton said he's been convicted for fraud."

"I suppose Cara's going to write an article about what a hothead I was tonight."

"She promised to be fair and accurate. Under the circumstances, it's the best we can hope for."

"Fair and accurate is still going to make me look like a hothead. I doubt that will help my case with the good people of Mustang County."

"The article probably won't help, but something

she brought up to me tonight might. What can you tell me about the scams your cousin pulled?"

Bart searched his memory. He'd tried not to pay too much attention to Kenny's dealings. Just thinking about them made his cheeks burn with shame that he and his cousin shared the same blood. "He was into everything from selling lame horses to spreading stories that local legend Shotgun Sally was born and raised on Jeb's ranch, the Bar JR."

"My friends Cara and Kelly like to talk about Shotgun Sally. Kelly is one of Sally's descendants." Her elegant eyebrows dipped low over those intense blue eyes. "How could Kenny profit from saying Sally was born on the Bar JR?"

"If there was a way, he found it. He sold worthless tin plates claiming they were from Sally's homestead. Tried to promote tours of Jeb's property. He even sold jars of dirt saying it came from Sally's grave."

"But that's all pretty harmless. Why was he charged?"

"After he gave up on cashing in on Shotgun Sally, he sold cemetery plots to old folks. A lot of cemetery plots. Only the plots weren't his to sell. He did three years in Huntsville. That was the end of his scams, far as I know. Though I'm sure he's still finding some way to make a quick buck."

"How far would he go to make money?"

He cocked his head at her question. "What are you thinking?"

"From the way he talked about his father, I assume they didn't get along."

"You assume right. Kenny had no use for Jeb. The only people Kenny blamed more than Jeb for his failures were me and my daddy."

"Because your father inherited more land?"

"Yes. And because my father was a success with the land he inherited. Jeb started with a nice cattle operation. It only took him about two years to drink it away." He could see where she was going. Her mind was heading down the same path his had since his run-in with his cousin. "You're thinking Kenny might have killed Jeb."

"I keep wondering how he knew your knife was the murder weapon."

"Unless he used it himself?"

"Is it possible? Would Kenny kill his own father if it meant a big inheritance?"

"I wish I could say no. But I wouldn't put it past him. If he inherits."

"He might not?"

"Like I said, there wasn't much love lost between them. Jeb might have written Kenny out of his will, for all I know."

"I'll find out. Our firm is handling the estate."

"And defending me. Isn't that a conflict of interest?"

"I'm not handling Jeb's estate. Don Church is."

Bart nodded. Donald Church was a specialist in wills and trusts and a full partner of Lambert & Church. Back before Bart's dad had gotten sick, he'd always sworn Don was the most honest lawyer in

Texas. Bart gestured ahead to the next turn off the highway. "You'll want to take a right up here."

Lindsey swung the car onto the road. Juniper groves flanking both sides, the drive twisted up a gentle hill overlooking the most beautiful country this close to Dallas/Fort Worth. Too bad it was way past nightfall. He would have loved to show her the view.

Still looking worried, she squinted her eyes at the road ahead. "How about that blonde with Kenny tonight? Who is she?"

"You got me. Last I kept track, he was dating Debbie West. But that was years ago. Before she married that other loser."

"Debbie West?"

"A girl who grew up on a ranch bordering the Four Aces."

"That blonde last night sure didn't look like the girl next door."

Lindsey was right about that. "She's built like the women Kenny usually goes for—long legs, lots of curves—but something isn't quite right."

"Like what?"

"Her clothes. Her attitude. She has too much class to be hanging around Kenny. Of course, anyone who saw you and me together might say the same thing."

She pulled her eyes from the road and gave him more than a quick glance. "What do you mean?"

"Look at you. Sophisticated, smart, a real lady yet sharp as a barbed-wire fence. If you weren't my lawyer, you'd never be hanging around an old cowboy like me."

"Says who?" A smile softened her pretty lips. "If I wasn't your lawyer—" She pressed her lips together and looked out the window, like she was embarrassed by the unprofessional blunder she'd almost made.

If she wasn't his lawyer...

Did she mean she would be interested if... Bart shook his head and smothered the hope sparked by her comment. It didn't matter. He sure as hell wasn't going to be doing much dating. Not where he was headed. If they didn't find some evidence they could use for a defense, the last thing he would have to worry about was his love life.

He looked at the white pipe corrals and sprawling ranch house, apartment building, bunkhouse and barns ahead. A red dually pickup stood parked in its usual spot next to the main horse barn. He tilted his watch to read the face in the dashboard glow. It was plenty late, but this was important. "Gary's home."

"Your foreman?"

"You said you wanted to talk to him?"

"Very much. If he didn't drive you home last night, maybe he knows who did."

LINDSEY FOLLOWED Bart around a metal pole barn and toward the ranch foreman's place. White buildings and a maze of pipe fence glowed in the moonlight and stretched as far as she could see. Even in the dead of night, the ranch was impressive. "Beautiful place."

"Wait until you see the whole thing in the daylight." He motioned to the barn they were circling.

"This is the horse part of the operation. It's my addition."

"Addition? Don't all ranches use horses?"

"People in these parts don't like to talk about it, but a lot of ranches rely on helicopters and four wheelers to move their cattle. With the cost of labor and the difficulty in finding qualified cowboys, it's more economical than using horses. And these days, we in the beef industry need all the economy we can get. We even have a helicopter here at the Four Aces."

"Do you use horses at all?"

"We use them most of the time. The helicopter just helps out. But most of the horses in this barn spend more time in the show ring than on the range."

"I used to show horses when I was growing up. Pony Club."

"No kidding? I'd like to take you riding."

"Do you have a hunt seat saddle handy? Or do your horses just ride western?"

"Honey, quarter horses can do everything worth doing. And you can bet my quarter horses can do it better than anyone else's." He turned and gave her a teasing smile.

Her heart lurched sideways. He was something, this cowboy. Proud as any red-blooded Texan one minute, yet self-deprecating the next. And through it all, his green eyes shone with a sparkle that made her wish...

She stopped herself. What would she wish? That she could toss her career out the window and fall into his arms? The arms of a client, for crying out loud?

She'd kept her focus solely on proving herself in

her career since she was eighteen. She wasn't going to let a little Texas charm turn her head now that she was on the cusp of proving herself. And saving him from a life behind bars.

Looking straight ahead, she focused on the long, low apartment building. On the other side of a large paddock, another good-sized building that appeared to be more living quarters perched on top of a gentle swell of land. And if she turned around, she knew she'd see the roofline of the main house. "This place is like a mini city. How many people live here?"

"Me, my daddy, my daddy's nurse, Beatrice, my foreman, Gary and eight full-time hands, more during roundup. Daddy and Beatrice live in the house with me. The others live in the apartment building if they have families, and in the bunkhouse if they're single or just here for roundup."

She looked at the low stretch of apartments. All the windows of the long building were dark. Except for the bark of a dog, the place was quiet as a tomb. "Is everyone gone?"

"Don't let the quiet fool you. After working from can't see to can't see, there's not much a body wants to do most days but eat and fall into bed. Come sunrise, this place will be hopping." He strode to the first apartment and rapped on the door. "Gary? You awake? I need a word with you."

No answer.

Bart knocked again. Still nothing. Finally he turned away from the door and shrugged. "Old boy's probably worn-out after doing my work today along with his own. And probably being raked over the coals by Hurley Zeller to boot. Guess we'll have to wait for tomorrow. I'll walk you back to your car.''

They'd just circled the barn when Lindsey spotted her car. It lurched at a strange angle. As if the tires on one side were flat. ''My car.''

Bart picked up his pace, long legs striding straight for the vehicle.

Lindsey half ran alongside to keep up. As they approached, her breath caught in her throat. Red spray paint slashed across the windshield and white hood, and dripped down like blood. *Stay away from the murderer or die.*

Chapter Four

Deputy Hurley Zeller leaned on the hood of Gary Tuttle's dually and picked his teeth with a dirty fingernail. "I still can't believe you called me all the way out here to report a prank."

Bart had been trying to reach Deputy Mitchell Steele all night. Finally, he'd given up and asked the dispatcher to send whoever was available. He wasn't surprised when Hurley showed up. Hell, he wouldn't be surprised if the little bastard had conspired to keep Bart from reaching Mitch—the only fair-minded deputy in the county.

Bart narrowed his eyes. He hadn't liked Hurley Zeller since high school. But after taking the brunt of the deputy's sarcasm and bad attitude since his arrest, he was damn close to hating the man. "Seems more like a threat than a prank, Hurley. The car won't start, either. Whoever did this took the distributor cap."

Hurley shrugged. "Committing murder will win a few enemies. For you and your lawyer."

Exactly what Bart was afraid of. He glanced at Lindsey. Despite her brave front, he could tell by the rigidity of her spine she was upset. "I want protection for Lindsey."

Lindsey stiffened. "I don't need protection. You're the one in danger."

Hurley scoffed. "You're both kidding, right? We ain't got enough deputies in Mustang County to haul all the drunks off the highways on Saturday night. We don't have the manpower for baby-sitting."

Bart forced himself to take a calming breath. Hurley might be right. It might be nothing. Whoever vandalized Lindsey's car had the opportunity to hurt them, after all, and hadn't taken it. But whatever the vandal's intentions, Bart wasn't taking chances. "Lindsey is a lawyer with Lambert & Church. I doubt Paul Lambert and Don Church would be happy if something happened to her. And last I knew, they were big political supporters of Sheriff Ben."

The grin fell from Hurley's lips. If there was anything the deputy believed in, it was keeping his boss happy. "Fine. I'll arrange for a car to drive by her place every hour or so."

Lindsey shook her head, her eyes shooting bullets at Bart. "I don't need protection. I can take care of myself."

"That may be, darlin', but I want to make sure." Bart glanced back at Hurley and nodded. "I'll let Paul and Don know you're handling the situation. Also, you might want to stop at my cousin Kenny's house and ask him where he's been tonight. And while you're there, keep your eye out for red paint."

Hurley looked like he wanted to spit. He turned and walked to his car.

"And another thing," Bart added.

Hurley stopped in his tracks. "Don't push your luck, Rawlins. I'm warning you."

"You wouldn't know what happened to my shotgun and hunting rifles, would you?" While waiting for the deputy to arrive, he'd gone into the house for his shotgun. He wanted to be able to protect himself and Lindsey in case the vandal decided to turn to more serious crime. But all he'd found was an empty gun case, its door gaping.

"We confiscated them when we searched the property this morning."

Lindsey's glower moved off Bart and onto Hurley.

The deputy nodded in her direction. "The warrant included all weapons. I'll get you a copy."

"You do that."

"When can I get them back?" Bart asked.

"After you've served your time in Huntsville. I guess that would be twenty-five years to life." Grinning, Hurley climbed into his car, slammed the door and hung an arm out his open window. "If you'd like, Ms. Wellington, I'll drive you back to town, make sure you're safe." He glanced at Bart with that damn grin, as if he expected points for the offer.

BY THE TIME Bart fell out of bed the next morning, it was almost five o'clock. If he wanted to talk to Gary before the foreman left for the south pasture, he'd have to hurry.

He showered, shaved, downed a cup of coffee and made it to the barn just as Gary was saddling his little bay mare. "Hey, Gary. Can I have a word?"

Face deeply creased by sun, wind and hard living, Gary Tuttle looked and moved like a man twenty years older than his forty-five. He tossed his prized saddle, which he'd won on the rodeo circuit when he was young, on the mare's back and squinted at Bart with tired gray eyes. "You're the boss."

Bart frowned. Gary had been like a big brother when he was growing up on the ranch. He'd taught Bart how to rope a steer from horseback, how cattle break when they're on the move and how to fly the ranch's Enstrom F-28F piston helicopter. He'd put so much work into the Four Aces, Bart's dad had given him a chunk of the place as a reward. But ever since Bart's dad had gotten sick, Gary was like a different man. Tired. Distant. And he'd talked more than once about retiring from the ranching business.

Bart had hoped a night together shooting bull at the Hit 'Em Again would bring back some of the brotherly camaraderie they'd lost. Unfortunately he didn't remember how his plan had turned out. "I suppose you heard about the goings-on yesterday."

Gary settled the saddle on the mare's back and flipped the near stirrup up. "Hurley Zeller told me you were arrested for killing Jeb. He asked me a bunch of questions."

"What did you tell him?"

"Nothin' much."

"I didn't do it. You know that, don't you?"

"If anyone deserved it, it was Jeb."

Bart shook his head. "As miserable as that son of a bitch was, no one deserves to die."

Gary flicked a shoulder in a half shrug. Avoiding Bart's eyes, he grabbed the cinch and fastened it around the mare's girth. She took in air, bloating her belly so he couldn't tighten it.

"I tried to wake you up last night."

"Oh?"

"I wanted to ask you about our night at the Hit 'Em Again."

"What about it?"

"How did I get home?"

"You blacked out, huh?"

"Something like that."

Gary kneed the little bay in the belly. Pinning her ears, she let out the air with a grunt. He pulled the cinch tight, slipped the latigo into its keeper and let the stirrup fall against her side. "When I went to leave, you were already gone. I figured you must have left with that fine young thing you were talking to at the bar."

"Fine young thing?"

"You would have to black out to forget her. Blond. Legs longer than this mare is tall. Former Dallas Cowboys cheerleader, according to your drunken babble."

The same blonde who was with Kenny in the alley? There couldn't be two long-legged mystery blondes in Mustang Valley. Had she been the one to drug his drink? Provided the date-rape drug was responsible for his memory loss. "Did you see me drinking whiskey?"

Gary shook his head. "Just beer. But I wasn't watching over you like a goddamned nursemaid."

Too bad. A nursemaid was apparently what he'd needed that night. Maybe he should have asked Beatrice, his daddy's nurse, to go to the saloon with him instead of Gary. "What else did I say about the blonde?"

"You were too busy to have much conversation with me. But I got the impression she was hitting on you and not the other way around."

At least he wouldn't be known around town as some kind of womanizer. Just a drunk and a murderer. "Who was she?"

"Don't know. But you might want to check out yesterday's *Mustang Gazette*. They put out a special afternoon edition. There's a picture of her in it with Jeb."

"You have one?"

Gary nodded toward the tack room.

Bart stepped inside. The scent of horse sweat mingled with well-worn leather. He spotted the paper laying on a saddle rack. Bracing himself, he picked it up and looked under the headline proclaiming Mustang Valley's second murder in two months. His gaze landed on a picture of his uncle. Thin-lipped mouth set at a mean angle, Jeb stared at the camera as if challenging it to a fistfight. And on Jeb's arm was the blonde who'd accompanied Kenny to the alley last night.

The jingle of spurs jolted him out of his surprise. He glanced up from the paper as Gary leaned in the tack-room door, holding his saddled and bridled horse by a single rein. "She's something, ain't she? Can't figure out for the life of me what she'd be doing with old Jeb."

Neither could Bart. But he was damn well going to find out.

LINDSEY LOOKED UP from her paperwork as Bart laid a copy of the *Mustang Gazette* in front of her. Propping a hip on the edge of her desk, he watched as if waiting for her reaction.

She had a reaction, all right, but it wasn't to the newspaper.

Dressed in a denim shirt, jeans, tooled belt complete with big silver buckle and a well-shaped straw hat that blended with the sun-kissed blond of his hair, Bart looked like a lonely woman's cowboy dream. And his scent. Mmm. He wore the rugged scent of leather, honest work and fresh air. She breathed deeply and struggled to keep her composure.

What was it about being around this man that made her lose her equilibrium? She'd felt off balance since the moment she'd first touched his hand in the jail's visiting room. His attempt to protect her last night after her car had been vandalized hadn't helped matters. It had only made her feel helpless on top of fluttery. An unwelcome reminder of the way she'd always felt when her parents and brothers had hovered over her as she was growing up—the way they would still be hovering if she hadn't moved halfway across the country. As if she were incompetent, helpless, dependent.

As if she were still a little girl.

She shoved her insecurities to the back of her mind and tried to focus on the faces in the newspaper photo. Her past feelings didn't matter. Nor did her attraction to her client. She was on her own now, and the chance to prove herself was right in front of her. All she had to do was reach out and grab it by the throat. "I saw the picture about ten minutes ago. I would have called, but I figured you were already on your way here to keep our appointment."

"I've never seen that blonde around Mustang Valley before. Suddenly she's everywhere."

She nodded and studied the woman's attractive features. "At least, everywhere with Jeb and Kenny."

"And me."

"You?" Adrenaline jolted through her bloodstream, partly due to surprise, partly due to something she couldn't quite put her finger on. "When was she with you?"

"I caught up with Gary this morning. He said she was sitting with me at Hit 'Em Again the night Jeb was killed."

"The same woman? Is he sure?"

He nodded.

Another jolt.

Jealousy. That was it. Plain, simple and inappropriate. She shook her head, trying to clear her mind, trying to reclaim her professional demeanor. "Does Gary know who she is?"

"Nope."

"I gave Wade a call at the bar this morning. He didn't remember seeing her at all that night. And neither did the kid he's training. Of course, the kid was concentrating so hard on serving drinks, he didn't remember much of anything." Lindsey bit her bottom lip. "Maybe the blonde's working with Kenny."

He tilted his head and waited for her to go on.

"Say Kenny did kill his father in order to inherit the ranch and he wanted to make it look like you're responsible. How would he do that? I mean, he could never get close enough to slip Rohypnol in your beer. Not without you being suspicious. But he could hire the blonde to do it."

"If Rohypnol was in my beer."

"I borrowed Cara's car to take the pieces of bottle to the lab this morning." She didn't want to think about what she would do if the drug didn't show up in any of the tests. She knew Bart was telling the truth about blacking out that night. And she knew he was innocent. She could feel the honesty in every word from his lips. But faith and trust weren't exactly accepted as evidence in a court of law. And as much as she didn't want to admit it, she wasn't an unbiased judge where Bart Rawlins was concerned.

No, she needed evidence. And she needed it now.

"There's one thing that bothers me," Bart said, his gentle mouth turning down in a frown.

Lindsey pulled her gaze from his lips and met his eyes. "What?"

"A scam like the one you're talking about would

take a lot of planning on Kenny's part. I'm not sure he has it in him.''

She didn't know Kenny Rawlins, but from the limited exposure she'd had to him, she was inclined to agree. "Okay. What if he didn't hire the blonde? What if she was the brains behind the brawn? It would explain how they know each other. It might even explain that picture of her and Jeb. She could have been setting him up for murder.''

Bart tilted his head, as if weighing her arguments, then nodded. "I could see that.''

"All we have to do is show a connection between Kenny and the blonde. And dig up evidence showing means and opportunity.''

"A tall order.''

It was. And at this point, it was pure speculation. But if they could find something concrete—

The sound of knuckles rapping on wood cut off her thoughts. "Come in," she called.

The door swung open and Paul Lambert popped his head inside. "Excuse me, Lindsey. I need a word with Bart.''

"Sure, Paul, come in.'' She waved him inside.

Paul Lambert was a year or so shy of sixty. But with the touch of silver at his temples, his casual confidence and his friendly brown eyes, it was no wonder Dot down at the sandwich shop chatted about him incessantly, even though he was married. But more important to Lindsey than his looks or confident air was the aggressive way he'd recruited her right out of law school. As if he truly believed she was capable of becoming the lawyer she wanted to be.

Paul crossed the plush money-green carpet that covered all the floors at Lambert & Church and held out a hand to Bart.

Bart gave it a firm shake. "What's up, Paul? You aren't here to ask me if I want to sell the Four Aces again, are you?"

Paul grinned. "Naw. I gave up hope years ago."

Lindsey glanced at Bart. "You aren't thinking of selling, are you?"

Bart shook his head. "Not a chance. It's kind of a joke. When my daddy signed over the ranch to me, not a day passed that Paul or Don didn't ask me if I wanted to sell."

"We weren't that bad. But if you've reconsidered, I do have a client who might be interested." Paul's grin widened.

"You'd be the first to know. Unless Don beats you to it."

"Speaking of Don, have you talked to him yet?" Paul's grin subsided, his business demeanor taking over.

"Don? I can't say I've seen him. Why?"

"Your uncle stipulated that your father be present for the reading of his will."

Bart took a step backward, his surprise evident. "You sure about that?"

"Quite sure."

Bart shook his head. His lips flattened into an ironic half smile. "When I was a kid, I used to hope my daddy and Jeb would work through their differences one day and bring the family back together. I should have known one of them would have to be dead for it to happen.''

''Do you think your father will be able to attend?''

''Daddy? Not a chance.''

Sympathy furrowed Paul's brow. ''I suppose his only brother's death is something of a shock.''

''I'm sure it would be, if I'd told him.''

''You haven't told your father?'' Lindsey sat up in her chair, surprise riffling through her. ''Why not?''

Bart looked at her, the sparkle in his green eyes muted by obvious pain. ''He hasn't been well.''

''I know he's sick, but wouldn't he want to—''

''He just lost Mama a year ago. He doesn't need to know.''

Paul cleared his throat, bringing their attention back to him. ''If you want to represent your father, I'm sure that would be in keeping with the spirit of the will.''

Bart shook his head. ''I won't be there, either.''

Lindsey bit her lip. Murder was usually committed for one of two reasons—love or money. Finding out to whom Jeb had left his possessions could serve to illuminate both his love life and his finances. ''It might be a good idea to attend.''

''Jeb didn't leave my daddy anything. And Daddy probably wouldn't want me to accept it if he did.'' Bart's gaze bored into her, as if he was trying to make her understand. Or simply get her to back off.

She returned the eye contact. Despite his discomfort, she couldn't back off. Not when so much was at stake. "But it might be interesting to see to whom Jeb *did* leave his possessions."

Bart glanced at the floor and pushed a stream of air through tight lips as if he saw her point. "I'll think about it."

Paul gave Lindsey an approving nod before turning to Bart. "Don has scheduled the will reading for Tuesday, three in the afternoon."

"That soon?" Lindsey asked.

Paul shrugged. "I know. It's a little irregular. But it's what Jeb wanted." His attention riveted to the newspaper laying on Lindsey's desk. To the photo of Jeb and the blonde. He looked away, the planes of his face hardening.

"Do you know her?" Lindsey asked.

"Who?"

"The woman in the photo with Jeb Rawlins?" She pointed to the paper.

Paul bent over her desk and studied the woman's features. He lifted his shoulders in a stiff shrug. "Can't say I do." He looked up from the paper, careful not to meet Lindsey's eyes.

An uneasy feeling skittered over her skin. Paul knew the woman. Lindsey would stake her career on it. But why would he lie? "I think she's involved with Kenny in some way."

Paul casually crooked a brow. "Hmm."

"She was with him last night at Hit 'Em Again. We thought maybe she was involved with Kenny in some of his scams."

He nodded but still didn't meet Lindsey's eyes.

"Before I forget, Nancy wanted me to tell you she has the files you wanted."

Lindsey nodded. The office administrator, Nancy Wilks, had promised to have an intern copy every file that had been subpoenaed by the prosecution to present to the grand jury. No doubt Lindsey had a late night ahead of her. "Thanks, Paul."

Paul nodded, glanced at his watch and focused on Bart. "I have to run. I have a meeting. I hope you reconsider coming to the will reading. You might find it illuminating."

As soon as Paul disappeared through the office door, Bart glanced at Lindsey. "That was strange."

Lindsey nodded. "Paul obviously knew who the blonde was. But why wouldn't he admit it?"

"Hell if I know. But I think you were right. I think I should probably go hear what Jeb put in his will." He let out a stream of air. "But I'll do it on one condition."

"What's that?"

"I want to bring my lawyer with me. I don't like to make a move without legal advice I can count on." A grin spread over his lips and a twinkle appeared in his green eyes.

She returned the smile despite herself. "I think that can be arranged."

He really was an amazing man. He seemed to know just what to say, just how to smile to disarm her. Yet his warm grin and unassuming phrases didn't seem like merely an attempt to manipulate her. They seemed true and honest and a genuine part of who he was.

"Do you need help toting those files Paul mentioned?"

"That would be great."

Feeling stronger and more confident than she had in a long time, she walked out the door and down the hall to the main office, Bart by her side. She had a lot of work ahead of her. She just prayed she would find something useful soon. Because if she didn't, a very good man would pay the price.

Chapter Five

Lindsey rubbed her eyes with her thumb and forefinger and glanced at the clock hanging on her kitchen wall. Almost eleven o'clock at night. For two days she'd been sorting through the files she and Bart had picked up, and she still hadn't found anything.

She trained her eyes on the paper in front of her. Figures from the last year Jeb had cattle on his ranch swam on the page. Number of head sold, maverick rate, shrinkage rate—a regular crash course in cattle ranching and none of it seemed to lead anywhere. Luckily Bart had spent a couple of hours explaining the terminology to her over dinner. If it weren't for him, she would really be lost.

As if finally gaining permission to go where it wanted, her mind latched on to thoughts of Bart. His honesty, his sincerity and his disarming smile.

The phone rang, cutting through her thoughts. She punched the Talk button and held it to her ear. "Hello?"

"Hey, Baby."

Lindsey flinched. All her brothers called her Baby.

When she was a kid, the name had made her feel special, like her four older brothers really noticed her. And cared. Now at the age of twenty-six, she'd re-evaluated. "What's up, David?"

"What's up? Why does something have to be up? Can't I just call my little sister occasionally?"

"If you, Michael, Rich and Cameron only called occasionally instead of every night, it might be nice. As it is, your calls are bordering on harassment."

"I'm just doing my part to save your career, Baby."

"My career doesn't need saving."

"Come on, Lindsey. You're a Wellington. You have a brilliant legal mind. Why waste it out in the sticks?"

His patronizing tone made her nerves stand on edge. "I'm not wasting anything. I'm making a career for myself. The same way the rest of the Wellingtons did."

"But you didn't have to travel halfway across the country to do that."

She blew a frustrated breath through pursed lips. She'd been through this argument countless times with each of her brothers. Even her mother and father chimed in on occasion. "I want to make it on my own. Why is that so hard for everyone to understand?"

"Maybe because we've given you an open invitation to join our firm here. In your home. And you won't be defending drunk drivers and reading real estate contracts on the side. Or you can clerk for Dad, specialize in constitutional law, work on what you care about. Hell, maybe someday you can make it to the bench. Follow in Dad's footsteps. That's what you want, isn't it?''

David knew darn well that was what she wanted. But that wasn't all she wanted. "I want to make it on my own," she repeated. "I want to earn my own way just like the three of you did when you started the firm from scratch. Like Cam did. Like Mom and Dad did in their careers."

"You don't have to do that, Lindsey. That's my point. There are advantages to you being so much younger than the rest of us. Mom and Dad are established in their careers now. We're all established. Why not cash in on that? We all respect you. You don't have to earn anything."

"You respect me? That's a new one. That must be why you don't trust me to make it on my own." David, Michael and Rich had started their own firm. Cameron had risen to the ranks of federal prosecutor. Her dad was now a judge. Even her mother had finished her degree and landed a job teaching law after years of raising a family.

"Come on, Baby. Not that whole 'make it on my own' thing again."

"Why shouldn't I make it on my own?"

"Because you don't have to."

He would never understand. None of her family would. They all wanted to take care of her. To protect her. To coddle the baby sister. To give her all the advantages they never had. Advantages they didn't believe she could earn for herself. "I don't have time to

talk about this, David. I have a big case I'm working on.''

''Don't tell me, a drunk driver who dented someone's pickup truck *and* ran over a dog?''

She set her chin and scowled into the phone. Maybe
in a way, she needed Bart as much as he needed her.
Because by proving his innocence, she would also
prove herself. To her family, to the world.

She just hoped she was as brilliant as her family
liked to think.

TRUSSED UP in a white shirt with pearl snaps and a
black tie to match his black Wranglers, Bart felt about
as uncomfortable as a boy dressed for Sunday school.
But he sure didn't feel like a boy around Lindsey Wellington. Far from it. Every glance from those intense
blue eyes made him feel all man.

Her baby blues bored into him now. ''Ready?''

He clapped his Resistol straw hat on his head and
forced his thoughts to the will-reading ahead. He
didn't know why he bothered dressing up. If the situation was reversed, he had no doubts Jeb would walk
in with tattered jeans and manure on his boots. But
somehow it didn't seem right to wear work clothes
while attending the only last rites a man would ever
have.

Not that any part of this felt right. ''I still don't like
this. I never wasted much time on good thoughts about
Jeb when he was alive. I feel like a damn hypocrite
suddenly showing up for the will.''

She pushed back her chair and stood. ''I know. But

your uncle put your father's name in his will for a reason. We need to know what it is. Besides, the last several nights I went over the files Nancy copied for me, and I found absolutely nothing. We need a break.''

Bart sighed. Good points. Not that Lindsey had to make them in order to convince him. Hell, he'd follow her anywhere. All she had to do was crook one of those ladylike fingers. ''Let's get it over with, then.''

With a decisive nod, Lindsey strode out the door of her office and led him down the hall.

Even though the annex fire, which had burned Andrew McGovern's body, had happened weeks ago, the scent of smoke still permeated the building. Especially in the area near the now-boarded-up entrance to the annex. Bart tried not to think about Andrew or the fire or the subject of murder as he swung through the open door of the conference room behind Lindsey and looked straight into the angry black eyes of his cousin.

''What the hell are you doing here?'' Kenny bellowed. He balled his hands into fists, as if threatening to take Bart on in the middle of the conference room.

A challenge Bart would be happy to oblige if they were back in the alley behind the Hit 'Em Again. ''I wouldn't be here if Paul hadn't asked me to come.''

Kenny threw a scowl in Paul's direction.

The firm's partner leaned against the table, his eyes moving over a file in his hands, clearly unfazed by the likes of Kenny Rawlins.

At the end of the long table, Donald Church, the other half of Lambert & Church, stretched to his full five-foot-and-a-sliver height and cleared his throat. Dressed in his usual starched white shirt, French cuffs and two-thousand-dollar suit, Don reminded Bart of a round little peacock the way he preened and strutted in his fancy clothes. But the man also had the warmest smile Bart ever remembered seeing. He turned that smile on Kenny. "I'm sorry, Kenny. I know it's hard to have Bart here. But Jeb stipulated that Bart's father attend this reading. And since Hiriam can't be here, Bart has agreed to take his place."

Kenny growled deep in his throat like a dog on the end of a fat chain. "The old bastard must have done it to torture me. One more kick from beyond the grave."

Paul tossed the file he was perusing onto the table and clapped a hand on Kenny's shoulder. "Have a seat, Ken. This will all be over soon enough."

Kenny sank into a chair, his glower still focused on Bart.

Bart couldn't blame him. If the situation was reversed, he'd probably be across that table with his hands around Kenny's throat before either of the partners could say their first cajoling word.

Turning away from Kenny, Bart grasped one of the chairs and pulled it out for Lindsey. Flashing him a small smile, she lowered herself into the chair and set her briefcase on the floor beside her. Legal pad in hand, she crossed her long legs and looked to Don, waiting for him to begin.

Bart folded himself into a chair beside her. The faint

scent of roses teased the air between them. He fought the urge to lean close and breathe her in.

Paul was the last to find a chair. Once he had, Don treated the whole table to one of his smiles and chewed over a long preamble about Jeb being of sound mind—which Bart had always doubted. Then he cut into the meat of the will. "To my only son, Kenneth B. Rawlins, I leave the case of whiskey in the basement of the house."

"Case of whiskey? He drank every drop of that a long damn time ago."

Don held up a hand. "I also leave him the contents of my safe-deposit box at First Texas Bank, Mustang Valley branch and my 1995 Ford pickup."

Kenny leaned forward in his chair. "What about the ranch? What the hell does it say about the ranch?"

Paul laid a hand on his shoulder. "Let Don continue, Ken."

Eyes drilling into Bart, Kenny grasped in his shirt pocket, pulled out a pack of cigarettes and shook one from the pack.

Flipping the cigarette between his lips with one hand, he searched his pocket for a lighter with the other. Finding a red Bic, he lit the smoke and took a deep drag.

Don blinked his eyes a few times and looked back down at the document in front of him. "I leave the acreage and buildings that make up the Bar JR ranch to—"

Bart shifted in his chair. He drew a breath and held it.

"—my brother, Hiriam Rawlins."

A wooden feeling crept through Bart's limbs. He glanced at Lindsey. Shock was written all over her face, the same shock that had him numbed from hat to boots. He forced his gaze to Don. "You've got to be kidding."

"It's all right here."

He shook his head, trying to cut through the sluggishness in his brain. "I don't believe it. It doesn't make sense."

"It all makes perfect sense to me."

Bart winced at the rasp of his cousin's voice.

Leaning back in his chair, Kenny's lips twitched into a smirk. He blew smoke from his nostrils, a thickening cloud circling his head.

Chapter Six

Back in her office, Lindsey set her briefcase on the desk and struggled to hide the anxiety threatening to overwhelm her. Judging from the look on Bart's face when Don had read Jeb's will, he was already unnerved. The last thing he needed was to see that his lawyer was struggling with worries of her own.

Bart sank into one of the chairs in front of her desk. Grasping his hat by the crown, he lifted it off his head and raked a hand through his hair. "Jeb's will doesn't make a lick of sense. Hell, if I didn't know the old coot better, I'd think he set me up and killed himself just so I would take the fall."

Her stomach clutched. "Is it possible?"

He blew out a frustrated breath. "Jeb was a miserable son of a bitch, but he wasn't suicidal. Not unless you count trying to drink himself to death."

Lindsey shook her head. "The facts of the case don't point to suicide anyway. Suicide victims don't slash their own throats. I guess I was just grasping at straws."

"The way things are stacking up, I'd give about anything for a few of those straws."

Lindsey gave a heavy sigh and leaned back against the desk. So much for hiding her apprehension. Not only was she grasping at straws, she'd just admitted it to her client. "Nothing has changed. We still have to find who had most to gain from Jeb's murder. And Kenny is still tops on the list."

"Maybe if he'd inherited Jeb's land. But he didn't."

"That doesn't matter. He probably didn't know what Jeb planned any more than you did."

Bart shook his head. "He knew. The thing I can't figure out is why he wasn't more angry about it. He was more upset about me being in the room than about the ranch going to me and my daddy."

Lindsey thought about the smirk on Kenny's face. Bart was right. Kenny knew. And he seemed more amused than upset.

Bart shook his head. "Why the hell would Jeb will the land to Daddy and me? He never cared much for me, and he outright hated my daddy."

"Would your father know why?"

Bart dropped his focus to the carpet. "No."

"Maybe it's something in their history. Maybe your grandfather made them promise to reunite the ranch when one of them died."

"If that's it, we'll never know."

"Why not?"

"My daddy…" He trailed off.

"Your daddy what?"

He shook his head. "Nothing. He won't remember, that's all."

She was pretty sure that wasn't all, but Bart obviously wasn't planning to come across with more. And without knowing more, she would have to take his word that asking his father was a dead end. "If only we knew how the blonde fit into all of this. Or if she fits at all."

"Maybe I could take her picture and ask around."

"That might tell us who she is."

Reconsidering his idea, Bart shook his head. "But it might also let Hurley Zeller know exactly what we're up to. And we still won't know how she fits in with Kenny's schemes."

"True." She tented her fingers and tapped them against her lips. "So what if we come at this from another angle?"

"What angle would that be?"

"Both Jeb and Kenny were clients of Lambert & Church, right?"

"As far as I know."

"Then what if we have a chat with the lawyer who handled Kenny's criminal case?"

"Can we do that? Isn't there some kind of attorney-client privilege?"

"For the lawyer's dealings with Kenny, there would be. But unless the blonde is a client of Lambert & Church, confidentiality doesn't extend to her."

"Who worked on Kenny's case?"

By the time the question crossed Bart's lips, she was already starting for the door. "Let's find out."

THE WAY OFFICE ADMINISTRATOR Nancy Wilks watched over the offices of Lambert & Church reminded Bart of a mother hen keeping tabs on her chicks. She clucked out orders to everyone from employee to partner. She fussed over each detail with motherly intensity. She even bobbed her head when she was upset. She was bobbing her head now as she sorted through a stack of file boxes, her severely cut dark hair swinging against her cheeks. "I swear interns these days have no idea how to file anything. I had a case last week where one filed a brief under the client's first name. Can you imagine?"

Lindsey gave her a nod and an understanding smile. "I have a question for you, Nancy."

"Can it wait until I straighten out this mess?"

"Actually, no."

Nancy dragged in a put-upon breath. "Let me find one thing, and I'll be all yours."

Despite the frustration crawling over his hide, Bart tried to hang on to his patience. No point in getting Nancy's back up. Besides, she seemed like a nice enough person, poultry tendencies aside.

He helped her shove around a few boxes, placing them where she directed. Finally she seemed to locate what she needed. Once she'd finished her business, she lit a cigarette and focused on Lindsey. "Okay, what can I do for you?"

"Do you remember Kenny Rawlins's conviction for fraud?"

"Sure. He was convicted for selling cemetery plots."

Lindsey nodded. "Who acted as his lawyer?"

"It had to have been Andrew. He handled all the criminal work back then."

Bart jolted. "Andrew McGovern?"

"He's the one."

"Damn." There would be no asking Andrew Mc-Govern about the details of Kenny's scam. Not since the mayor had murdered him a month ago.

Lindsey let out a sigh that echoed with the same frustration that wound in Bart's gut. "Thanks, Nancy."

"That's it?"

"That's it. Good luck straightening out the filing system."

"Thanks. It looks like I'm going to need it." She took a drag off her cigarette like she was preparing herself for the ordeal ahead.

They walked back to Lindsey's office. As soon as they stepped inside, she closed the door behind her and turned those intense blue eyes on him. He could see the wheels turning in that pretty head.

"When I came to Lambert & Church, I took over Andrew's old office and he moved to the annex."

Bart nodded and waited for her to continue.

"He was busy with cases and I was busy studying for the bar, so it took forever to complete the move."

"And?"

"When he died and the annex burned down, some of his personal papers were still in my office."

"Do you have them?"

"No."

He let out a breath.

Lindsey held up a finger, a smile spreading over her lips. "I gave them to his sister, Kelly."

He nodded, his pulse breaking into a jog. Kelly McGovern Lansing wasn't only Andrew's sister, she was Wade Lansing's new wife…and Lindsey's friend.

Lindsey grasped the cordless phone from her desk and punched in a number. She gave Bart a little smile as she listened to the phone ring. "Kelly? It's me, Lindsey. Do you still have those notes of Andrew's I gave you a couple weeks ago? I need to take a look at them, if you don't mind."

IT DIDN'T TAKE Lindsey long to tie up her business in the office. And when Bart offered to give her a ride to Kelly's, she didn't argue. The garage had left a message while she was attending the reading of Jeb's will. They'd replaced the distributor cap and tires, but the new paint job would take longer to complete. Unless she wanted to drive through town with red spray paint slashed across the hood, she wouldn't have a car until tomorrow. Tonight she was stranded. Or she would be if it weren't for Bart.

He pulled the truck to the curb of a little house nestled on a quiet Mustang Valley street and threw it into Park. He climbed from the cab and circled to the passenger side. He held out a hand as Lindsey pushed her door open.

A little feminine shiver rippled through her at the touch of his callused fingers. She gritted her teeth. Wouldn't her brothers love this? Her client helping her from a truck as if she wasn't capable of jumping down herself?

Even so, she had to admit she liked the way Bart held doors open for her, helped her from his truck and took off his hat when she entered a room. She liked the roughness of his fingers and the gentleness of his touch. She liked the scent of fresh air and leather that emanated from him, more seductive than any cologne. As a matter of fact, there seemed to be nothing she *didn't* like about the cowboy.

And that's what drove her craziest of all.

Once her foot hit pavement, she pulled her hand from his grasp and stood on her own two feet. "Thanks for the ride. Kelly said she'd give me a lift back to my apartment."

"I can wait until you're done."

She drew another breath. As much as she wanted him to stay, she knew she needed to be away from him now. She needed to be on her own. "Not necessary. Kelly said she's dropping by Hit 'Em Again later to pick up Wade. My apartment isn't far out of her way. Really."

"All right. But if you get in trouble, I expect you to use that little cell phone of yours to give me a call."

She couldn't keep the tension from creeping up her spine at his words. But if there was anything she'd learned while dealing with her brothers' protective streaks all these years and with Bart's the past couple of days, it was that she could tell him she'd be fine on her own until she was hoarse and it wouldn't make a difference. He would still hover. He would still worry. He would still believe she couldn't take care of herself. "I'll call if I need you."

"Promise?"

"I promise."

"And if you learn anything from the files—"

"You'll be the first to know."

A grin spreading across his face, he circled to the driver's door, climbed into the truck and waited until she entered the little house.

As soon as Lindsey stepped inside, Kelly, wearing a Hawaiian shirt that set off the blue of her eyes, swept her upstairs. "It took some digging, but I found Andrew's papers."

"Thanks, Kell. I owe you one."

"Don't be silly. What are friends for?" She shook her blond head and waved Lindsey into the master bedroom. Sparsely furnished with only a bed and a single dresser, the room was stacked with open boxes. "I'm still moving in. With everything that's happened and the wedding and Wade training Jerry to run Hit 'Em Again while we're on our honeymoon, we haven't had much time to unpack."

To Lindsey's amazement, Cara, the newshound, sat among the boxes in the middle of the floor, a folder open in her hands. A stack of folders and legal pads perched on a box next to her, obviously already perused. She looked up at Lindsey through her red curls. "Hey, Lindsey. Have a seat. These are a lot more interesting than trying to decide what image Kelly should project on her honeymoon."

Lindsey's stomach clenched. She shot Kelly an alarmed glare.

Kelly held up her hands in front of her as if to ward off the look. "She was here when you called. She helped me dig out the box. She had to look at the notes. You know Cara."

Lindsey knew Cara, all right. That's what had her worried. "You can't write about anything you've found in that box."

"Why not?"

"Have you ever heard of attorney-client privilege?"

"Have you ever heard of freedom of the press?"

"Have you ever heard of getting me in a lot of trouble at the firm? Maybe even with the state bar?"

"They aren't official legal files, Lindsey. Just Andrew's private notes."

"Depending on what's in them, they could be classified as attorney work product."

Cara closed the file in her hands. "I never thought of it that way. I'm sorry, Lindsey. I'd never do anything purposely to get you in trouble."

Lindsey plunked onto the floor beside her friend. "I know."

Kelly sat cross-legged beside them. "Cara got the papers from me, and I'm not bound by any kind of attorney-client privilege. Doesn't that count for anything?"

"Not really, since I gave them to you in the first place." Lindsey looked at the stack with dismay. There was no sense in being upset with Cara or Kelly. The situation was her fault.

"Hey, it's understandable, Lindsey," Kelly said. "The past few weeks have been tough for all of us."

Especially Kelly. She'd found the man of her dreams, but she'd also lost her brother. Lindsey laid a supportive hand on her shoulder.

Cara tapped the folder in her lap. "I won't write about any of this unless I can verify it through another source. And at that point, who's to say where I uncovered the idea originally?"

Lindsey nodded. Cara wouldn't violate her ethics any more than Lindsey could violate her own.

"Are we all friends again?" Kelly asked.

Lindsey looked at the two women next to her. She'd had friends back in Boston. But those friendships had mostly been based on family ties and political influence. Her friendships with Kelly and Cara weren't like that. Even though the two of them had been buddies since childhood, as soon as they'd met Lindsey, they'd opened their arms to her without reservation. And since then, the threesome had formed a strong bond simply because they liked and respected each other. Friendship for friendship's sake. "Of course we're friends."

"How about a hug then?" Kelly reached out her arms.

They rose to their knees, put their arms around each other and hugged. When they finally sat back on the floor, all three had tears in their eyes.

Cara was the first to recover. "Well, now that we have that out of the way, let me show you what I found." She reached for a file marked *Rawlins,* flipped the manila cover open, pulled out several pages and handed them to Lindsey.

Lindsey skimmed the pages. "These look like stories."

Cara nodded, her eyes bright. "Local legends, actually. Most of them are about Shotgun Sally."

Lindsey remembered Bart mentioning that Kenny had tried to pass off the Bar JR as Shotgun Sally's original homestead.

"Here. You've got to read this one." Kelly plucked one of the legends from the pile and slipped it in front of Lindsey's nose.

She started to read. In the legend, Shotgun Sally was a lawyer back when women weren't yet allowed to join the Texas bar. When a cowboy named Zachary Gale was wrongly accused of murder, Sally stood up to defend him when no one else would. And she fell in love with him. Believing in him and laying her life on the line, Sally finally saved Zachary from hanging. And at the end of the story, married to the cowboy she loved, Sally became the first female lawyer to officially pass the Texas bar.

"Sounds a little like you and your good-looking cowboy, Bart Rawlins, don't you think?" Cara's eyes twinkled with humor.

Heat crept up Lindsey's neck and pooled in her cheeks. She remembered the look Cara had given her and Bart in the alley. If her attraction to Bart was that obvious, she was in trouble. "That's ridiculous. He's my client."

"Client, schmient. He's hot." A teasing smile

curved Cara's lips. "Maybe even hot enough to tempt *you* into his bed?"

"Cara!" Lindsey protested. Her cheeks felt like they'd burst into flame. She never should have confessed to her friends she was still a virgin. That she'd been so busy focusing on her career she hadn't had the time or interest to get involved with a man.

"Don't mind Cara. She's a hopeless matchmaker," Kelly said.

"Hey, I was right about you and Wade, wasn't I?"

Kelly gave Cara a knowing half smile. "Yeah. Even though it took a shotgun to convince him." The two of them broke into laugher.

Lindsey shook her head. She still couldn't believe Kelly had held a shotgun on Wade to get him to agree to marriage—as if he'd really needed convincing. Lindsey was lucky she wasn't defending Kelly in court, too.

"It was Shotgun Sally's blood in me. And now I'm a saloon owner just like Sally." Kelly grinned and lowered one eyelid in a playful wink. "A saloon owner by marriage, anyway."

Lindsey frowned. "I thought Shotgun Sally was a lawyer."

"Actually—" Cara piped in "—she was an investigative reporter. All the other things she did were just covers so she could get her scoop."

"Now you've really confused me."

"Look." Cara spread the pages out on the floor. "There are a dozen or more Sally legends, all of them different. But in each one Sally gets her man, Zachary Gale, and metes out justice on her own terms.''

Lindsey nodded. ''On her own terms. I can identify with that ambition.''

''See? You've been bitten by the Shotgun Sally bug already.''

Lindsey looked down at the legends covering the bed. Legends Cara had pulled from a file marked *Rawlins*. ''Did you find the legends in that folder originally?''

''Yeah.''

''Why would Andrew keep them in a folder marked *Rawlins?*''

''I wondered that same thing,'' Cara said.

Kelly shrugged.

Lindsey flipped open the file's cover. The rest of the folder seemed to be filled with scribbled notes about the Bar JR. ''It doesn't make sense. Unless…''

''Unless what?'' Kelly asked.

''Bart said Kenny Rawlins tried a few get-rich-quick schemes to cash in on the Sally legends.''

Cara nodded. ''I remember. It was before his cemetery plot scam.''

''Could the legends have something to do with that?''

Cara tilted her head and regarded the folder. ''Maybe. But the rest of the notes don't have anything to do with Kenny's scams.''

Kelly compiled the legends into a stack. ''Maybe they were just misfiled. Andrew was a wonderful lawyer, but no one in her right mind would describe him as organized.''

Lindsey nodded. Maybe Kelly was right. Maybe the legends had found their way into the file through nothing more intriguing than sloppy filing.

''I might know someone who can answer your questions,'' Cara said. ''One of the professors at the community college specializes in local folklore. Della Santoro. If there's any kind of a connection between the Sally legends and the Bar JR or Kenny Rawlins, she would know. You can meet Kelly and me for lunch tomorrow and then I can take you down to the campus and introduce you.''

''That would be great, Cara. Thanks.'' Lindsey took the papers from Kelly and stuffed them back in her briefcase. At least she had a direction.

''No problem. But you have to repay me by answering one question.''

Lindsey groaned. ''Cara the investigative reporter rears her ambitious head again.''

Cara smiled, unfazed. ''What were you hoping to find in these files? I know you want to find some dirt on Kenny Rawlins, something to show he killed old Jeb, but what *specifically* are you looking for?''

Lindsey sighed. It probably wouldn't do any harm to tell Cara. And maybe her friend could help. ''Off the record?''

''Of course.''

''The blonde with Kenny in the alley the other day was also in the bar with Bart the night Jeb was killed. And she was hanging around Jeb before his death. I hoped Andrew's notes could tell me how she's connected.''

''You mean Brandy Carmichael?''

''I know Brandy,'' Kelly said.

Brandy Carmichael. So that was her name. ''I thought there was a chance she'd been involved with Kenny in his past scams.''

Cara frowned. ''I doubt it. Unless the scam had something to do with real estate.''

''Real estate?''

Kelly nodded. ''Brandy is a real estate broker. She has her own company in Dallas. I met her when I was toying with the idea of going into real estate after college.''

Lindsey nodded, her mind whirring with possible implications of this new information. ''Thanks. I should have known I could count on you guys.''

Kelly grinned. ''Like I said before, what are friends for?

BY THE TIME Kelly dropped Lindsey off at her apartment, it was well past ten o'clock. Except for the low rumble of CNN coming from the open window of one of the ground-floor apartments, the building and surrounding landscaped grounds were silent as death. Other than the news junkie, Lindsey's fellow tenants in the mid-priced eight-unit had either not realized it was one of the rare June nights that was cool enough to do without air conditioning, or they had turned in early to catch some sleep before work the next day.

Letting herself into the glassed-in foyer, she turned

and waved to Kelly, who was waiting at the curb for Lindsey to get safely inside before she drove away. After collecting her mail from the locked box in the foyer, Lindsey climbed the stairs, unlocked the door and slipped into her apartment.

The air was dead and stuffy. Setting her briefcase on the floor and her mail and cell phone on the telephone table in the little alcove just inside the door, she eyed the blinking light on her answering machine. She hit the Play button. Sure enough, there was a call from her brother Cam. Add the call David made to her at work, and that qualified as a call from each of her four big brothers in the past two days. A full-scale barrage. No doubt it would be Mom and Dad's turn to call her tomorrow.

After erasing the calls, she walked to the sliding glass door overlooking the quiet street below, opened it a crack and breathed in the fresh air. There was nothing like fresh air to remind her of all Mustang Valley offered that she couldn't find in Boston. It wasn't that her brothers and parents didn't want what was best for her. The problem was they assumed only *they* could provide it. That she couldn't find it on her own. That she couldn't make it without help.

She strode into her bedroom to change into the New England Patriots T-shirt she always slept in. Slipping the red-white-and-blue-logoed shirt over her head, she laughed. Maybe she'd even trade it in for Dallas Cowboys sleepwear. That would be sure to get her brothers' goat.

And she could imagine the smile on Bart's face.

Cara's comment about Bart tempting her into bed teased at the back of her mind. She shook her head. She couldn't let herself think about Bart as anything but a client. If she wanted to prove herself, she had to confine her thoughts to the framework of his case.

After washing her face and brushing her teeth, she padded back into the living room to lock the patio door before she went to sleep. She had another long day ahead. Hopefully her meeting with Della Santoro and an investigation into Brandy Carmichael's real-estate business would yield results. If not, she didn't know where to turn.

She closed and locked the sliding glass door. She had just flipped off the lights when a thud caught her attention.

Her heart lodged in her throat.

Someone was in her apartment. Someone—images of paint, red as blood, flashed through her mind. She had to get out of here. She had to call for help.

As quietly as she could, she padded for the door. If she could wake one of her neighbors, use their phone—

A dark shadow lurched toward her from the alcove.

Panic shot through her. She threw up her arms, trying to protect herself, trying to fend off the assault.

Something hard and flat hit her.

She stumbled backward, grabbing the wall to keep herself from falling.

Another blow landed against her head.

She hit the phone table and crumpled to the floor, mail scattering on the tile around her.

Chapter Seven

Lindsey curled into a ball on the cold tile, her arms shielding her face. Her pulse thundered in her ears. She was afraid to move, afraid to breathe.

The shadow loomed over her. A man. He clutched her briefcase in his fist.

She braced herself for another blow.

But instead of hitting her, he spun and bolted for the door. Throwing it open, he dashed into the hall. Heavy footfalls echoed the length of the hall and down the stairs. The thump blended with the frantic beat of her heart.

He could have killed her.

She struggled to her feet. Her legs wobbled. Her stomach rolled. Grasping the wall, she struggled to rein in her panic.

The table in the little alcove lay on its side. The mail she'd gotten from her box was scattered upon the floor. The telephone lay next to her cell phone. And judging from its broken casing, her answering machine was history.

Her briefcase. It was gone. The intruder had hit her

with it and taken it with him. Was that what he was after? Was that why he'd broken into her apartment? She didn't buy for a moment that this was a simple burglary. He hadn't gone near the television or expensive stereo equipment her brothers had given her for a passing-the-bar gift. He'd sneaked into her apartment for something specific. And as far as she could tell, the only thing he'd taken was her briefcase.

Hands shaking, she picked up the cell phone. She needed to call the sheriff's office, tell them someone had broken into her apartment, attacked her, stolen her briefcase. But somehow she couldn't force her fingers to punch 9-1-1. She couldn't deal with Hurley Zeller's cruel laugh and mind games. Not when she was feeling so vulnerable. Not when she was feeling so weak.

Bart.

He'd told her to call if she needed him. And she needed him now. Needed to hear his voice, needed to see the strength in his eyes, needed his warm arms to fold around her and stop her from shaking.

She found his number in the Mustang Valley directory and punched in his number with trembling fingers. The line rang, pulsing in her ear.

Finally his sleepy voice answered. "Hello?"

"Bart—" A frightened sob stuck in her throat and cut off her breath.

"Lindsey? What's wrong?"

Her mind whirled with relief, with fear, with confusion. She struggled to find the words to tell him what had happened—struggled and lost. "I—I need you."

"I'll be right there."

BART HADN'T HIT ninety on the highway leading to Mustang Valley since he was seventeen and driving his dad's old Ford pickup. But he buried the needle now.

The fear in Lindsey's voice when she called had hit him like a kick to the gut. Her voice had sounded so small, so vulnerable, so afraid. His first response had been to get to her as fast as he could, to pull her into his arms and make her safe. His second was to kill whomever had made her sound that way.

He roared onto Main Street and checked his speed. Thank the good Lord, the town's sidewalks rolled up by nine o'clock during the work week. Once he passed Hit 'Em Again, the street was clear until he made the turn that led to Lindsey's apartment complex.

The street outside her building was quiet. No deputy in sight. Damn that Hurley Zeller. If he'd been protecting Lindsey like he'd promised—

Bart shook his head, cutting off the thought. It didn't matter what Hurley was up to. Bart was here now. And he'd damn well make sure Lindsey was okay. And that she stayed that way.

He pulled to the curb, switched off the engine and threw open the door. Boot heels echoing on pavement, he dashed to the front door and hit the doorbell button next to her last name.

"Bart?" Lindsey's shaky voice filtered through the speaker.

Relief tumbled through him. "It's me, darlin'."

"Second floor, apartment B." She buzzed him in.

He raced to the top of the stairs and found her door. She opened it before he had the chance to knock.

Her face was pale and she clutched the doorjamb for support. But she wasn't bleeding. She wasn't hurt.

Bart stepped into the apartment and gathered her into his arms.

Her body trembled against him. Her arms tightened around him. She felt as substantial as a flower, as delicate as a petal. Her lips pressed against his neck, right above his shirt collar. "I know I should have called the sheriff, but I just couldn't."

"I'm here. I've got you." He rubbed his hand over the length of her back and kissed her hair. "Tell me what happened."

"Someone broke into my apartment. When I spotted him, he hit me with my briefcase and ran."

Rage twisted in Bart's gut. What kind of a coward would hit a woman? If he got his hands on the son of a bitch— He forced himself to take a deep breath. "All I know is, I'm awful glad you're okay. You could have been killed." His voice cracked. His chest tightened. Even hearing those words come from his own lips was too much.

Lindsey pulled back and looked up at him. Her eyes locked with his.

He smoothed her satin cheek with his fingers, wanting to reassure himself she was all right. Wanting to feel her, to smell her, to draw her in. Tilting her head back, he lowered his head and fitted his mouth to hers.

She tasted like warm honey and smelled like roses. He pulled her closer, joining his tongue with hers, soaking in the feel of her, the heat of her, until he was drunk with the contact.

He'd wanted this so much. Ever since she'd walked into the county jail with that classy lift to her chin and raw determination in her eyes. She was his lawyer. He was accused of murder. Nothing could ever come of this, but he wanted it all the same. Wanted the heat of her, the taste of her. Wanted to hold her in his arms and be her hero.

He wanted Lindsey.

And she needed him. She circled his neck with her arms, pulling him closer, deeper into the kiss. Her thighs brushed against his.

Heat shot straight to his groin. What he wouldn't give to carry her to bed, strip her clothes off and run his hands over every inch of that smooth skin. He stepped farther into the apartment, pulling her with him. Something crunched under his boot.

He drew back from the kiss and looked down. A smattering of letters and a mail-order catalog were strewn across the floor. A battered answering machine lay on the tile, its plastic casing in shards under his feet.

A groan of pleasure died in his throat. What was he thinking? Lindsey was attacked here tonight. She could have been hurt. She could have been killed. She needed him, all right. But not to kiss her, not to make love to her. She needed him to keep her safe.

He looked up, peering into the intense blue of her eyes. ''Pack your things.''

A little crease formed between her elegant eyebrows. "My things?"

"You're moving out to the ranch."

THROUGH THE ARDUOUS process of filling out a police report about the break-in and the long drive to the Four Aces Ranch, Lindsey tried to silence the nagging voice of doubt whispering in her ear.

The effort was a waste of time.

She'd moved to Mustang Valley to be self-sufficient, to build a career and a life on her own, and she'd already blown it. Big-time. She might be able to take care of herself when her life was well ordered and predictable, but as soon as something out of the ordinary happened, she needed a big strong cowboy to save her.

And Bart Rawlins was definitely the man who fit that bill.

She stared at the lines of fence and juniper groves whizzing past the truck window, drew in a deep breath of fresh country air and tried to purge memories of his strong, safe arms and passionate kiss from her mind.

It was no use.

But even though his arms had sent a thrill through her body as strong and jolting as an electric shock, and his kiss had caused her whole system to overheat, she couldn't let the sensations short-circuit her mind. She was a lawyer. A professional. And Bart was her client. She had fallen into the role of damsel in distress tonight, but that didn't mean it would happen again. And even though she'd agreed out of fear to stay at the Four Aces Ranch, nothing had changed. She wanted to kiss him. Heck, she wanted more than a kiss. But she hadn't gotten where she was by giving in to sexual attraction every time it heated her blood. She would handle her attraction to Bart the way she'd always handled the appeal of sexy men. By ignoring it.

The truck passed under the archway proclaiming the Four Aces Ranch and rattled through the open gate designed to keep cattle inside. Lindsey glanced at Bart, his face illuminated in the dashboard's glow, his head bobbing slightly in time with Merle Haggard on the CD player. She looked ahead at the sprawling white house and ranch buildings crowning the top of the hill. The ranch was as quiet as the last time she'd visited. All the lights in the apartments, barns and the bunkhouse were dark. The only sign of life was a single light blazing from the main house.

As if following her gaze, Bart's eyes flicked over the house before landing on her. "Someone must be up."

"Your father?"

"Or Beatrice."

"The nurse?"

Nodding, he swung the truck into the driveway leading to the house and pulled in front of the garage. Switching off the ignition, he turned to her. "It's been a rough day. Let's get you settled so you can get some sleep."

He climbed out of the truck and circled behind.

When he joined her at the passenger side, he was carrying her suitcases. She held out her hand for them.

He looked down at her open palm. "Don't be ridiculous. What kind of a man would I be if I let a lady carry her own bags?"

"I can do it."

"I know you can. But that doesn't mean I'm going to let you." He strode away, leaving her to catch up.

The main house was a rambling affair, the kind she'd seen on television westerns. The long roofline was broken by half-a-dozen dormer windows. On the main floor, double-hung windows peered out on a wood porch that ran the length of the structure.

Bart led her to a side door instead of continuing down the porch to the main entrance. "I'd bring you through the front door, but around these parts, the only people who use them are the politicians."

"The only thing worse than lawyers."

"Damn straight."

She followed him inside, smiling. She liked that he took her through the door he regularly used himself.

The door opened into a utility area connected to the kitchen. As soon as they stepped inside, a rough voice echoed through the dark hall. "Where's my money?"

Lindsey followed Bart into the kitchen. Although a light glowed from somewhere deep in the house, this room was dark. He flicked on the light. At the table sat a man almost as tall and probably once as strapping as Bart. But time had obviously taken its toll on his body, leaving him bony instead of lean, worn instead of vital. He frowned at Bart, confusion pinching his bushy gray brows. "Who the hell are you? Did you steal my money?"

Bart walked over to him and laid a gentle hand on his shoulder. "Your money is in the bank, Daddy. It'll always be there, whenever you need it."

"Then give it to me. I can't even buy a newspaper around here."

Bart glanced at Lindsey. She remembered him mentioning he hadn't told his father about Jeb's death. He probably didn't want him to see a newspaper, either. The last thing the older man needed was to read in a headline that his brother was dead and his son was accused of his murder. Especially if he was confused in the first place.

"I'll get you a newspaper, Daddy."

Bart's father looked at him with blank eyes, as if his demand for a newspaper had already slipped away. "Where's Abby?"

Bart's lips tightened with obvious pain. "Mama is gone."

"When she gets back, tell her I need more socks."

"I will." He smiled and patted his father's shoulder. "Daddy? This is Lindsey. She's a friend of mine."

The older man squinted at her.

"Nice to meet you, Mr. Rawlins." She held out a hand to shake.

He stared at it, as if he didn't know what the gesture meant. "This morning Abby made me scrambled eggs. I love scrambled eggs."

"That was Beatrice," Bart corrected, his voice patient.

"Who?"

"Beatrice. Your nurse. She's the one who made you the scrambled eggs."

"Abby makes the best scrambled eggs."

Bart sighed. "Mama always knew just how to take care of you, didn't she?"

"I'm tired."

"Why don't you go back to bed then? What were you doing sitting in the dark anyway?" Bart looked down a long hallway on the other side of the spacious family room. "Is Beatrice here?"

His father stared at him. "Who the hell is Beatrice?"

"Somebody has to get you to bed." Bart let out a heavy sigh and glanced at Lindsey, as if asking her to excuse him.

She nodded her go-ahead.

He helped his father up from the table.

"I'll take him, Bart." A soft Southern accent drifted through the room. Standing at the mouth of the hallway was an equally soft-looking woman. Pleasantly plump, with gray hair framing a wide face, the woman shuffled into the room in a blue housecoat. Her sharp blue eyes focused on Lindsey.

"Lindsey, this is Beatrice."

Lindsey returned the woman's smile. As soon as they exchanged introductions and pleasantries Beatrice looped her arm around Bart's father and ushered him down the hall.

Bart turned to Lindsey. "Now let's get you upstairs."

"It must be tough for you."

He looked at her like he had no idea what she was talking about.

"Him not remembering you. It must be tough."

"Sometimes. Truth is, he hasn't remembered me for a long time. I'm kind of used to it."

"He has Alzheimer's disease, doesn't he?"

A muscle in Bart's cheek flinched. He lowered his eyelids and nodded.

"I'm sorry."

He swallowed hard and shook his head. Stepping to the table, he picked up the suitcases. "Let me show you where you'll be staying."

She could understand his reluctance to talk about his dad. Just seeing Hiriam Rawlins tonight, she could get a sense of the man he used to be. The man who was fading away bit by bit. But she couldn't truly understand the pain of watching that horrible disease ravage someone she loved. She hoped she would never truly understand that.

She rose from her chair and followed Bart up the stairs to the second floor. The hallway ran the length of the house, at least a half-dozen doors opening onto it. "This house is huge. How many bedrooms are up here?"

"Five bedrooms, two baths. And there are two bedroom suites downstairs."

"Do you have a lot of brothers and sisters?"

"Nope. Just me. My parents wanted a whole houseful, but after I was born, my mama couldn't have any more. I always hoped I would fill these rooms with kids someday.'' A bittersweet smile flickered over his lips before he turned and walked halfway down the hall.

Lindsey followed, Bart's yearning and regret ringing in her ears.

He halted at a closed door. Using his elbow, he pushed the door open, then stepped to the side so she could enter. The room was spacious and airy. The yard light streamed in through two oversize dormer windows dressed with a pretty chintz fabric. Between the windows, a wide bed stood, piled with pillows and covered with a handmade quilt of the same chintz. Sweet and comfortable and just a little feminine. Even though the room was worlds apart from the sleek, contemporary house she grew up in, it felt like home. ''It's beautiful.''

''My mama. She could have decorated for one of those fancy home magazines, I swear.''

''I bet she could have.''

Bart shifted his feet, boot soles scuffing on the hardwood floor. There was pain in his mother's memory, too. So much sorrow.

''How did she die?''

''Doctors say it was heart failure.''

''And you don't believe the doctors?''

He didn't answer.

''What do you think it was?''

''It might sound sappy, but I'd say her heart broke.''

Her own heart pinched. ''Your father's illness?''

He set her suitcases down and plucked his hat from his head. He ran his fingers over the brim as if intent on checking its shape. "She always believed he'd get better. Like if she waited long enough and loved him hard enough, the disease would give up its hold. I think when it became clear he was never going to improve, she lost the will to go on."

The sadness in his voice seeped into her soul. She ached to wrap her arms around him, to hold him, to kiss him, to make his pain go away. The way he'd held her earlier tonight until she'd stopped shaking. The way he'd kissed her until his strength had made her whole. She barely stopped herself from reaching out to touch him. "I'm sorry about your parents," she whispered lamely. "I'm so sorry."

He pressed his lips together in a sad smile. "Me, too."

"I wish I could do something."

"You can't. No one can." Leaning forward, he fitted his hat on his head and peered at her from under the brim. "I'm glad you're here, Lindsey. And I'm glad you're safe. If you need me, I'll be in the next room."

The next room. Images bombarded her. His broad chest naked. His long, bare legs tangled in the sheets. His strong arms open and waiting for her to crawl into them. She took a deep breath and ruthlessly pushed the visions from her mind.

But she couldn't push away his quiet anguish over his father's illness and his regret for the empty bedrooms he'd hoped to fill with children. Nor could she banish the ache she'd seen in his eyes as he told her of his mother's death. And his mother's love.

She might be able to fight her physical desire for him. She might even be able to ignore it. But she couldn't ignore his vulnerability. His decency. The real man with secret dreams and secret pains. She closed her eyes and willed herself to stay rooted to the spot.

"Good night." His low drawl washed over her like a warm Texas breeze.

She summoned a deep breath. "Good night."

She didn't open her eyes, not when she heard his footfalls move into the hall, not when he closed the door softly behind him. It was only when he was safely on the other side of that oak barrier that she allowed herself to stare at the door.

Staying at the Four Aces was going to be harder than she'd ever imagined.

Chapter Eight

The morning sun stretched through the kitchen window and fell on the side of Lindsey's face, making her skin and hair glow with the soft light of an angel. "More coffee?" She held up the pot.

Bart tore his eyes away. Picking up his cup, he thrust it toward her. God knows, he needed the caffeine. Though he couldn't say if his lapse into staring had more to do with his sleepless night or the awe that something as exquisite as Lindsey Wellington was under his roof.

"I talked to the sheriff's office this morning about the break-in at my apartment."

"Let me guess, the deputy in charge of the case is Hurley Zeller."

"How did you guess?"

He blew out a disgusted breath. "And did he find anything?"

"Not yet."

"Don't hold your breath."

She gave him a somber smile. "How early did you get up?"

"I look that tired, huh?" He concentrated on watching her graceful hand pour steaming coffee into his cup.

"You should have woke me. I would have helped with chores. I have plenty of experience feeding horses and mucking stalls."

"Pony Club, right?"

She smiled. "How early?" she repeated, as if the answer was important.

"Sunrise. Not any earlier than usual." Hell, who was he trying to kid? He had gone out to the barns around sunrise, but he hadn't fallen asleep all night. He'd spent the hours listening for Lindsey's quiet breathing in the next room and wishing he was in that big bed alongside her, instead of hunkered down in his own room. Alone.

"Is your father up yet?"

"He usually sleeps late and through anything. Especially when he's been knocking around the house in the middle of night." He glanced down the hallway that led to his dad's rooms. When he turned back to Lindsey, she was watching him intently. As if she could see straight through him and into his heart. He forced a chuckle. "So how are we going to keep my hide out of prison today?" He meant the comment as a joke, but the words fell like a roped-and-tied calf.

"Cara's taking me to visit an expert on local folklore after she and Kelly and I have lunch."

"Local folklore? Am I missing something?"

She filled him in on the Shotgun Sally legends she, Cara and Kelly had discovered in Andrew's files. But though she didn't seem to be holding back any of the details, the way blood tinged her cheeks when she mentioned the legend about Sally as a lawyer suggested otherwise. "After we talk to her former professor, Cara will take me to the garage to pick up my car. It's supposed to be ready today. But do you have time to drive me into town this morning?" She flinched as she asked, like the question caused her pain.

"I'd be glad to give you a ride. Are just you and Cara going to the college?" Damn. He'd meant to make the question sound innocent, but his concerned tone left little mystery to what he was really thinking. And how worried he really was.

She raised her chin. "I'll be safe. Cara is one tough cookie. And I'm no pushover myself. If anyone messes with us, we'll make him wish he was never born."

"I don't doubt you will." He forced another chuckle, though he was far from convinced. He did know one thing, though. Lindsey Wellington didn't like him worrying about her. Not one damn bit. Too bad backing off wasn't in his nature. "What else are you planning for today?"

Lindsey eyed him warily. "I found out who the blonde is."

He crooked his brows and waited for the punch line.

"Her name is Brandy Carmichael. Cara and Kelly said she's a Realtor. She has a company in Dallas."

"A Realtor? Interesting."

"Interesting that Paul insists he doesn't know her."

He nodded. "It also makes me wonder if Jeb was planning to sell before he died."

"I thought I'd ask Brandy that very question."

"Are you planning to do that with Kelly and Cara?"

"Kelly is getting ready to leave on her honeymoon tomorrow morning. And Cara has work to do. I can't take up all of her day."

The tension was back in his gut. "You planning to go by yourself?"

That pretty chin raised back up a notch.

Tough. "I'll meet you at your office after lunch. We'll go see Miss Brandy together."

Lindsey opened her mouth to protest, then closed it without uttering a word. As if she could tell arguing would do no good. Especially when Bart had only to point to the break-in at her apartment last night to make his case. Finally she nodded. "Okay. After lunch."

"After lunch." Only a few short hours, but it seemed like an eternity. An eternity where anything could go wrong. At least he never promised he wouldn't be early.

"ARE YOU OKAY?" Blue eyes wide with concern, Kelly looked at Lindsey like she might keel over at any moment.

"I'm fine," Lindsey said in what she hoped was a casual tone. Resisting the urge to touch the scuff on her chin, she filled her friends in on the events of the night before, keeping her voice low so none of the other patrons at the diner could overhear. "The whole ordeal scared me more than anything."

"No wonder." The news of the intruder in her apartment last night even seemed to shake Cara. "You should have called us. You could have spent the night at my place. Where did you sleep? You didn't stay in your apartment after that attack, did you?"

Lindsey had contemplated not telling her friends for fear of worrying them. But she'd discarded that idea before Dot had brought their drinks. Friends didn't hold things back from one another. Not important things in their lives, such as this. And truthfully speaking, Lindsey needed to talk to someone about last night. She could discuss the intruder with Bart, but she could only talk to her friends about the rest of the night. "I called Bart Rawlins on my cell phone. He came over."

"And?" Cara prompted.

"He took me back to the Four Aces. I spent the rest of the night there."

A grin broke over Cara's lips. "Hot dog!"

Kelly smiled, shaking her head. "He rescued you? How romantic."

Despite the conflicting feelings waging war inside her, Lindsey couldn't keep the smile from her lips at her friends' enthusiasm. She had to admit last night had seemed like an unreal dream. The intruder. Bart's arms around her, keeping her safe. Going back to the ranch with him. It didn't seem like it really happened until this moment—when she told her friends.

Cara smiled over her drink. "I told you, Lindsey. I know about these things. You should listen to me."

"I hate to disappoint you two, but I slept in an extra bedroom. Nothing happened."

"Too bad," Cara said. "You've got to be more aggressive, Lindsey. Though I doubt Bart will need much of a push. Maybe if you just wander over to his room in the middle of the night. Tell him you were looking for the bathroom."

"Yeah, and do it naked."

"Kelly!" Now Lindsey's cheeks were burning.

"Oh, don't act so offended, Lindsey." Cara was grinning ear to ear. "You want him, that's obvious. So why don't you go for it?"

Cara was half right. Lindsey wanted Bart more than she'd ever believed she could want a man. But she couldn't go for it. For many reasons. "He's my client, for one thing."

"Maybe you have a bit of Shotgun Sally in you, too," Kelly said in a singsong voice.

Cara nodded, her eyes brightening the way they always did when she talked about one of her favorite subjects. "That's right. In the story where Sally is a lawyer, she saves her love, Zachary Gale, from hanging."

"Maybe it's fate," Kelly added. "The Shotgun Sally legend repeating. Maybe you're meant to be together. He keeps you safe, and you save his life. All the while, falling deeply in love."

Lindsey shook her head at her friends' romanticism. Part of her might want to believe every word they were saying, but the other part was rational. And focused. "I came to Mustang Valley to prove I could make a career—a life—on my own. I've only been here a few weeks and I'm already depending on a man to take care of me. No matter what kind of romantic twist you two give the situation, it's not what I want. I might as well have stayed in Boston under my brother's protective wings."

Kelly shook her head. "Your brothers and Bart Rawlins are not the same."

Cara nodded. "You can say that again. Nothing against your brothers, since I've never met them, but I don't think Bart is protecting you out of some sense of brotherly responsibility. Or because he doesn't think you can take care of yourself. I think he wants to jump your bones."

Lindsey almost groaned at the teasing, but that would give Cara too much satisfaction. Besides, she could accept the sexual attraction explanation far more readily than talk of fate and true love. So instead of protesting, she nodded her head. "And I want to jump his bones, too. But I can't. Not unless I want to undermine everything I've come to Mustang Valley to build—my independence, my career. So what do I do now?"

Both Kelly and Cara looked at her, as if this time neither had a quick quip or a piece of advice to give. Finally, Kelly spoke up. "I guess you just wait and see what happens."

Cara nodded. "And get Bart acquitted. No matter

what happens, you can't fall in love with him or jump his bones if he's behind bars.''

CARA AND LINDSEY made it to the community college right after Professor Della Santoro's lecture ended. They caught the professor outside one of the square, institutional-looking buildings that made up the Mustang Valley Community College campus.

"Cara. It's so nice to see you." Professor Santoro cradled a stack of books in one arm. She reached up with her free hand to brush back a strand of dark hair that had escaped from the neat bun at her nape.

Cara gave the professor a fond smile. "It's nice to see you too, Della. I've been meaning to ask you to lunch again. Maybe next week?"

"I'll check my calendar. What brings you here today?"

Cara nodded to Lindsey. "My friend Lindsey Wellington. She has a few questions about local legends, and I told her you were the one to ask."

Della Santoro scrutinized Lindsey through silver-framed glasses perched on the end of her nose. "I'd certainly love to help, if I'm able. What local legends are you interested in?"

"Shotgun Sally."

The professor shared smiles with Cara. "Our favorite," the professor said. "And perhaps the most controversial legendary figure in the area."

This was the first time Lindsey had heard of any controversy surrounding Sally. "Controversial? How so?"

"Because there are so many different versions of the Shotgun Sally legend, many people believe she never really lived. That she was actually a composite of many different women."

"But you don't believe that."

"There is ample evidence that she lived. Whether she did all of the things in the legends is another question. The most important thing about Shotgun Sally is that she represented a role model for women in an age where women weren't encouraged to do things like take part in cattle drives or own businesses."

"Or be lawyers," added Lindsey.

"Or muckraking reporters," said Cara with a smile.

Professor Santoro nodded. "Exactly."

Sally was a noble figure, indeed, real or composite. But that didn't address the questions Lindsey had come to ask. "What I'm really interested in is how she's tied to the area. Specifically whether she has anything to do with Jebediah Rawlins, his son Kenny, or the Four Aces Ranch."

The crease deepened between the professor's thin brows. "I'm not sure what you're looking for."

Lindsey gave her a quick description of Andrew's notes about the Bar JR and the legends found among them. "Is there anything that would explain why the legends would be inside that file?"

"As far as I know, Shotgun Sally has no direct link to the Rawlins family."

"Or the land?"

Tapping manicured pink nails on the books in her

arms as she walked, Professor Santoro shook her head. "I'm sorry. I don't know what else to tell you."

Cara let out a sigh. "I guess Kelly was right. It must have been a misplaced file. Or it had something to do with Kenny's penny-ante Shotgun Sally scams."

Frustration settled like a cold lump in Lindsey's stomach. Everything related to this case seemed to be a dead end. And although she really didn't have cause to hope a few legends stuck into Jeb's files had any real significance, she had let herself hope. It just showed how desperate she was.

They reached a low office building at the far end of campus. Della Santoro paused at the base of the steps and motioned to the glass doors with her free hand. "I have office hours now. You're welcome to come in and continue our chat. If you have any other questions, I'd be glad to try to answer them."

Lindsey gave the professor a grateful smile. She'd already wasted enough time hoping a few legends were the key to Bart's case. There was no point in wasting more. "I appreciate the offer, but I'm sure you're plenty busy. Thank you so much for your time."

After Cara also thanked her friend, the professor continued up the stairs and through the door of the building. Lindsey and Cara walked back to Cara's car.

Tilting her curly red head, Cara studied her. "Sorry."

Lindsey forced a shrug. "If there's no connection, there's no connection. I knew it was a long shot."

"What are you going to do next? Off the record."

"Bart and I have an appointment to talk to Brandy Carmichael. I want to see if her connection to Jeb is merely a false lead, too." If it was, Lindsey didn't know what she'd do next.

BART GUIDED HIS TRUCK into the circle cobblestone driveway and eyed the huge white stucco house perched on the tiniest scrap of land he'd ever seen. He glanced at Lindsey sitting in the passenger seat. "I don't understand it."

She furrowed that beautiful brow and looked at him questioningly. "Don't understand what?"

"People who shell out money for a house like this. It might be big and ritzy, but if they flex their elbows, they're in danger of poking their neighbor in the ribs."

She laughed, the musical sound filling the truck's cab. She grabbed the handle of the truck's door. "On that note, let's go in."

Bart frowned at the empty horseshoe driveway. "Are you sure she's here? I don't see a car."

"Her office said she's here. She's supposed to be getting ready for a broker's open house." Lindsey nodded to the red sign in front of the house with the name Brandy Carmichael and Associates printed on it in fancy letters.

"All right." He dismounted from the truck and circled to Lindsey's side. When he reached her, she was already jumping down from the runner. He had to content himself with steadying her when her heels hit the pavement.

They walked to the door together, Bart slowing his

stride so he could stay close beside her. Even in the outdoor air, he could smell the scent of roses. It wasn't strong. Not like some women's perfume. Lindsey's scent was subtle, classy. Like the woman herself.

They reached double front doors so grand he felt as small as an awkward boy standing in front of them. He looked around for a side door, but there wasn't one to be had. Not surprising. Anyone who would live in a house with no land to call his own and no connection to the earth that spawned him had probably never used a side door in his life.

Lindsey extended a graceful finger and pressed the bell. A gong sounded from inside. The sound was followed by the clack of heels on marble floor and the door opened.

Brandy Carmichael peered out at them. She looked older than she had in the alley that night, but still every inch the cheerleader. Her bouncy blond hair glistened in the afternoon sun. Red lips stretched into a smile, parting slightly to show the whitest teeth Bart had ever seen. "If it isn't Bart Rawlins and his lawyer…" She paused, waiting for Lindsey to fill in her name.

"Lindsey Wellington."

"Lindsey, of course." Brandy stepped back and swung the door wide. "Don't tell me, you're looking for a house."

Lindsey looked the woman straight in the eye. "We'd like to ask you a few questions."

Brandy's smile didn't fade as she motioned them into a white marble foyer as big as Texas Stadium. "Come inside. Please."

They obliged. She led them through the stadium and into a room with a view of the neighbor's pool. She motioned to a couple of white chairs and perched on a white stool next to a bar that had probably never served something as working-class as a plain old beer. Brandy turned on her smile. "So Lindsey, how are things at Lambert & Church?"

Lindsey lowered herself into one of the chairs and crossed smooth legs. "Are you familiar with my firm?"

"Let's just say there's a history."

Just what they were looking for, a history. Hopefully fraudulent and including Kenny. Remaining on his feet, Bart focused on Brandy. "What kind of history?"

"I know Don Church and his wife. And, of course, Paul Lambert." Her voice ran huskily over Paul's name. She shot a sly woman-to-woman look in Lindsey's direction. "Though I can't say I know his wife."

"That's interesting. Because Paul said he doesn't know you."

Brandy's smile seemed to grow wider and more slinky. "Not surprising, considering the circumstances of our many meetings."

"The circumstances?" Lindsey prodded.

"It's a long story. A long, *personal* story. And one I'm sure he doesn't want his wife to know about."

So Paul had had an affair with the ever-fetching Brandy. No wonder he didn't want to own up to knowing her. Bart glanced around the house's interior. "Might as well tell your story. It doesn't look like the good people of Dallas are lining up to buy this monster.''

"Some of the top real-estate agents in the area are joining me for cocktails. And don't worry. Once they get a look at this monster, as you put it, they'll be falling all over themselves to tell their clients about it." She lowered one made-up eyelid in a sexy wink and didn't volunteer more.

Just as well. Paul's sordid love life wasn't what they were after anyway. But Brandy's, on the other hand, might yield some answers. "How about Kenny Rawlins? Is there a long, personal story behind your relationship with him?"

"Not as long and not personal at all, thank God."

Lindsey raised a skeptical brow. "The two of you seemed pretty friendly in the alley behind Hit 'Em Again the other night."

"Appearances aren't everything. Listen, I play up to potential clients. That doesn't mean I sleep with all of them." Brandy tilted her head, her smile still in place. "Not Kenny Rawlins, at any rate."

"So he's a potential client?" Lindsey said, not missing a beat.

"I have a buyer who's interested in obtaining a large piece of land in the Dallas/Fort Worth area. The Bar JR fit the bill."

Lindsey nodded. "And Kenny wanted to sell?"

"He and Jeb wanted to sell. I wanted to accommodate them."

A piece fell into place in Bart's mind. The explanation for the photo in the *Mustang Gazette*. Brandy schmoozing a sale. "So what did this accommodation include?"

She frowned like she'd bitten into a sour apple. "Not what you're thinking."

He was thinking murder. But he doubted that was what she was talking about.

"I wanted to list the ranch before my buyer got it in his head to approach Jeb directly. That's it."

"So you want us to believe you were hanging around Jeb, and later Kenny, just to get a listing?" Lindsey asked.

"That's right. If I were a man, you wouldn't even question it."

Lindsey's elegant eyebrows lowered as if she was considering Brandy's statement. "So why were you playing up to Bart at Hit 'Em Again the night Jeb was murdered?"

Brandy turned her white smile on Bart. "That was for pure pleasure."

Lindsey stiffened.

Bart watched Lindsey out of the corner of his eye. After their kiss last night, he'd like to think her reaction to Brandy's quip meant she was jealous. But try as he might, he couldn't see a reason why she should be. Lindsey was so far beyond Brandy's league, it was like comparing Emmitt Smith in his prime to some skinny high school kid who couldn't make junior varsity.

"Of course, Kenny assumed the same thing you're assuming—that I'd sleep with him to get the listing."

She shuddered slightly. "It wasn't until after he realized I wasn't going to that he came clean."

"Came clean?" Lindsey prodded.

"He admitted the Bar JR wasn't his problem."

Bart must not have heard her right. "His *problem?*"

"That's right." A smile of realization spread over those red lips. "You don't know, do you?"

"Know what?" Lindsey asked.

"That the Bar JR is mortgaged to the hilt. That the cash you'd get from selling it wouldn't even come close to paying off the debt old Jeb ran up on the place."

The news hit Bart with the force of a mule kick to the head. No wonder Jeb had left the ranch to his dad and him. It made perfect sense. Jeb didn't want to reunite the original ranch. He wanted to saddle them with the tab for the past twenty years of his miserable life. And he knew Bart and his dad would pay that tab rather than give up the land. Bart shook his head, a grin tweaking his lips despite himself. "That crafty old buzzard."

Lindsey focused like a laser on Brandy. "Kenny told you this?"

Brandy nodded. "He laughed about it. Thought it was a big joke that Jeb planned to shift his debt to his brother when he died."

"Why would he tell you this?"

She shrugged. "Once he realized a roll in the hay didn't come with the listing, I guess he wanted to show me how stupid I was for hanging around him when he was dead broke."

"And when did this happen?"

"I don't know. A day or two ago. After Jeb was murdered." Brandy glanced at Bart.

Lindsey leaned forward, bringing the woman's attention back to her. "Was it before yesterday?"

"Before yesterday? You mean, did he know he wasn't going to inherit the ranch before the will was read?"

"Did he?" Bart asked.

"He told me about it the day after the murder. Right after we ran into the two of you in that alley behind the bar. He said you were as stupid as me." She gave a dry laugh. "Nice guy, your cousin."

The mule kicked again. Kenny was a nice guy all right. And now they couldn't prove that nice guy had any reason to kill Jeb.

Beside him, Lindsey seemed to droop. She held out a hand to Brandy. "Thank you for your time."

"No problem. Say hello to Paul for me, would you?" She winked again. "Oh, and Don, too."

After Bart shook Brandy's hand, as well, they left the mansion and started walking back to the truck. Bart's gut churned with acid. "So much for our notions about Kenny. If he knew the ranch was worthless and he knew he wasn't going to inherit it anyway, he had no reason to kill Jeb. Other than the fact that Jeb was a miserable old bastard and the world would be better without him, of course. But everyone in town had that motive."

"Not so fast." Lindsey stopped in her tracks and turned wide eyes on Bart.

Bart's muscles tensed the way they always did when he sensed the cattle were about to make a break for it. "What?"

"If you are convicted, what would you do with the Four Aces?"

"I suppose I'd have to sell. Gary is aching to retire from the ranching business. So without me, there would be no one to run the Four Aces. Besides, I'd need the money to take care of Daddy."

"So you'd sell the ranch and put the proceeds in a trust for your father?"

"That's how Don set up my will if I died, so I guess that's how I'd have him handle it if I was convicted, too."

She pressed her lips together, deep in thought. "And if something were to happen to your father before you went to trial?"

His tension ratcheted up a notch. "I suppose I'd still have to sell the Four Aces."

"And the Bar JR?"

"Daddy's will leaves everything to me." Maybe her point was as clear as the broad side of a barn, but he couldn't see it. "Even if I was convicted and something happened to my daddy, both ranches would just go back to me."

"The Four Aces would."

"But not the Bar JR?"

"That's what I'm telling you. If you're convicted of Jeb's death, Texas law says you can't inherit Jeb's land."

That barn was broad, all right, and it was staring

him in the face. "Then the Bar JR would go to Kenny. And by the time I came to trial and was convicted, Jeb's debt would already be settled."

She nodded.

Dread plowed into Bart's gut. "But he would only get his hands on the Bar JR if I was convicted...and Daddy was dead."

Chapter Nine

"Daddy!" Bart raced into the kitchen with Lindsey on his heels. Lindsey had used her cell phone to call the house and barn numbers repeatedly on the hour drive from Dallas. No one had answered. Still, he'd hoped by the time they'd gotten to the ranch, Beatrice would be back from a simple grocery shopping trip, his father in tow.

No such luck.

The house was dead quiet. No sign of his father. No sign of Beatrice. He raced down the hall to his dad's bedroom, his boots thundering on the wood floor. Maybe he'd find him taking an uncharacteristic afternoon nap. Maybe all his worry was for nothing.

He threw open the door. In the dim light, he could see the plain, dark spread smoothed over the bed. Untouched since morning. He spun around and started for the bathroom. "Daddy?" He pounded on the door, the wood trembling under his fist. "Daddy? Are you in there?"

No answer.

He turned the knob and pushed the door open. Holding his breath, he looked to the floor first.

White tile gleamed back at him. A quick glance around the empty room yielded nothing. No body, no blood, no Daddy.

He crossed the hall and knocked on Beatrice's door. No answer there, either.

"Maybe Beatrice took him somewhere," Lindsey said from behind him. "The doctor's office? The barber? Did she say anything to you or write his schedule on a calendar?"

Bart forced his mind to slow down. He had to concentrate. "I don't know. I don't remember." Damn him for not keeping better track of what his father was doing.

"You've had a few things on your mind. Like being accused of murder."

"That's no excuse. If anything happens to Daddy…"

"Can you reach Beatrice? Does she have a cell phone? Someone who would know where she might be?"

What was wrong with him? Why hadn't he thought of that before? "She doesn't carry a cell phone. But she does have a sister."

He found a phone and a phone book and punched in the number.

On the other end of the line, the phone picked up on the second ring. "Hello?" Beatrice's sister's cigarette-roughened voice carried over the line.

"Mary. It's Bart. Is Beatrice there?"

"Bart? Why would Beatrice be here?"

"Because she's not here. And neither is my dad."

"You're at the Four Aces?"

"Yes."

"Odd. Beatrice said she was going to be home all day. In case I wanted to call and chat."

Bart's heart froze. "Are you sure about that?"

"Yes, I'm sure. What's going on, Bart? You're scaring me."

He was scaring himself, too. His dad was confused, weak, helpless. He couldn't fight for himself. Hell, he didn't even know who he was half the time. And Beatrice. She was missing, too. Pressure bore down on his head until he thought his skull would split. He managed to mumble a few reassurances to Mary and dropped the phone into its cradle.

Lindsey touched his arm. "We'll find them."

"If anything has happened to my daddy and Beatrice, I'll kill Kenny with my bare hands."

"Do you want me to call the sheriff?"

"Would you?" As if it would do a damn bit of good. Hurley Zeller was more concerned about convicting Bart than finding the truth or protecting the public. And Sheriff Ben was too busy starting his campaign to replace the mayor to do his current job. He handed her the phone and headed for the door. He couldn't rely on the sheriff. He had to do everything he could to find his dad and Beatrice. And he had to do it now.

Bart reached the barn just as Gary and a new hand rode up. He flagged the foreman down. "Daddy's gone. Did you see anything the last hour or two? Anyone creeping around the house that shouldn't be?''

A stricken look spread over Gary's face. "Kenny."

Bart's pulse raced. "You saw Kenny?"

"I ran him off. About the time you left for town. I can't believe he'd do something to your daddy."

"Your daddy? Older man, a little shorter than me?" Tall, thin and strong as a steel fence post, the new hand riding with Gary wasn't old enough to grow a mustache. Though from the look of it, he was giving it a damn noble attempt.

"Did you see my daddy?"

The kid used his tongue to tuck his chaw into a cheek and spat into the dirt. "I seen an old man east of here when I was out looking for strays. Down by Shotgun Creek."

Bart lunged forward. "Wearing jeans and a—" He paused and tried to picture what his dad had been wearing this morning. "Blue button-down shirt?"

The kid nodded. "And a Dallas Cowboys cap."

That was him. It had to be. "Was anyone with him?"

The kid shook his head.

"He was alone?"

"Far as I could tell. He acted kind of strange. Said he didn't need or want my help. Called me Jeb."

"That's him." Wandering by himself. Maybe someone hadn't kidnapped him. Maybe whoever was behind this just let him out of the house and let his dad's confused mind do the rest. But if that was the case, what had happened to Beatrice? "What time did you see him?"

"'Round noon, I guess."

Just after Gary saw Kenny at the ranch. Damn. His daddy could have wandered miles by now. Bart focused on Gary. "How many hands are here right now?"

"Three, counting me and Billy. The rest are vaccinating calves in the south pasture."

Only three. Not enough to do a sweep of thirty thousand acres, that was for damn sure. "Take the horses down to the creek and look around the spot where Billy here saw him last." Bart glanced at the helicopter setting out on the ranch's makeshift helipad.

"You taking the Engstrom?" Gary asked.

"Damn straight. Is it topped off?" Bart had used the helicopter in the south pasture this morning to round up cows and their new calves for vaccinations.

Gary nodded. "It's ready to go. But there's supposed to be a storm west of here, moving in slow."

Bart checked the horizon. Sure enough, the dark shadow of rain clouds topped the gently rolling hills. "Then we'd better get a move on. I sure as hell don't want Daddy wandering out there in a thunderstorm."

Gary nodded again. "I'll get the other hand." Gary set a spur into his mare's side and sent her loping for the corral. Billy followed on his big gelding. They'd be out on the range before Bart got the helicopter's engine idling.

He strode for the helipad. He always kept the copter in working order, fueled up and ready to go, whether they were using it to gather cattle to pasture or not. Even after spring roundup, he had to search for breaks in fence and monitor the streams and rivers running through the pastures during summer droughts. And you never knew when an emergency might crop up.

Like now.

Lindsey raced out of the house and joined him at the helipad. "A deputy's on his way."

"One of the hands saw Daddy wandering toward Shotgun Creek a few hours ago. No one was with him."

"So he wasn't kidnapped?"

"Doesn't appear so. Someone just let him out of the house and watched him disappear." Anger and dread mixed with the nausea swirling in his gut. "He'll never remember how to get back to the house."

"What about Beatrice?"

"No sign of her."

"I told the sheriff she was missing, too."

"Good." Bart tried to push away his worry. He sure as hell hoped the sheriff could find her, because he didn't have the first idea where to look. He directed his thoughts to his daddy out on the range. Helpless. Probably afraid. Bart had to find him.

He climbed into the helicopter and started the engine. It roared to life, the sound bouncing off nearby barns. Overhead, the rotor was still, the engine only idling at the moment.

Eyeing the craft, Lindsey set her chin, circled to the opposite side and opened the door.

What she intended suddenly came clear to Bart. "Where do you think you're going?" he yelled above the roar.

"With you."

He shook his head. "Stay here. The hands went with Gary to look for my daddy. You need to wait for the sheriff."

She held up her little phone. "I'll call and fill him in about the cowboy seeing your father by the creek." She punched in the number and did just that as Bart performed a hurried series of safety checks. After turning off the phone, she climbed into the chopper.

Bart glanced at the storm on the horizon before turning a frown in her direction. "You can't go with me, Lindsey. It's not safe. Flying a helicopter is dangerous in the kind of weather that's blowing in."

"You need help."

"No."

Her eyes sharpened. "You don't want me staying here by myself, do you? Kenny or whoever let your father out on the range might still be around."

He pressed his lips into a line. Damn. He knew she was playing him, but the hell of it was, she was right. He couldn't leave her at the ranch alone. "You don't give up, do you?"

"Not when I know I'm right."

He looked out at the dark horizon. Sucking in a breath, he forced himself to nod. "Strap yourself in."

She fastened her safety harness. Glancing at her, he slipped on his headphones and motioned for her to do the same. Then he started the rotors.

He increased power, set the antitorque pedals and centered the cyclic. As he increased power further, the helicopter began to lift off the skids. He made more adjustments and brought the craft up about eighty feet into a hover. Scanning the horizon, he moved the cyclic forward and headed in a different direction from where Gary and the hands rode out. It was just a guess, but if Daddy had called the kid Jeb, there was a chance his mind had gone back to his childhood. That might mean he was doing something he and Jeb loved to do as kids. And exploring the banks of the Brazos River topped the list. It was worth a shot anyway. Bart was damn short on other ideas.

And on time.

He tapped Lindsey on the shoulder and pointed to a set of binoculars he kept in the craft to spot stray cattle or broken fence. She grabbed them and raised them to her eyes. Bart trained his own eyes on the land ahead of them. Swells of grassland stretched to the horizon. In the middle of the land, the Brazos River slithered between hills like a silver snake.

His dad was down there. Lost. Confused. They had to find him. Before the storm rolled in. Before he hurt himself.

Before it was too late.

A flash along the dark horizon caught his eye. He studied an ominous storm cloud. Another bolt of lightning followed the first. Judging from the way the cloud blotted out the afternoon sun, it wasn't a gentle storm. Not a storm he should be flying a helicopter into, that was for damn sure.

And not a storm a confused old man should be wandering around in alone.

They flew low, skimming over the ground at about a hundred feet. Over prairie and creek, woodland and river. Bart pointed out groves of mesquite, so Lindsey could study them more closely. In some spots, the scrub trees grew so thick it would be easy for a cowboy to lose half-a-dozen steers behind a thicket of gnarled branches, let alone one man.

"There he is." Lindsey's voice reverberated in his headset. She pointed to a rough area near the river.

He followed her outstretched finger. Sure enough, a small blue speck was picking his way through rock and mesquite. Bart scanned the area for a place to set down the helicopter. The top of the swell, before the land sloped to the river, was his best bet. From there, they would have to backtrack, fighting through scrub to reach his dad. It would take time, but he had no choice. They couldn't land on mesquite. He moved the cyclic in the direction of the swell.

A light flickered inside the craft.

Heart jolting into his throat, he looked down. The fuel-pressure light glowed orange.

Adrenaline flooded his bloodstream. He cut back on the cyclic and reduced pitch. Too late. Another sound sent his pulse pounding like a stampede of cattle—the sound of the engine sputtering and stalling.

Chapter Ten

Bart's pulse beat in his ears, louder than the slowing rotor of the helicopter. He kept the craft in perfect working order at all times. He knew he had fuel. He hadn't just taken Gary's word for it, he'd checked. It didn't make sense that the fuel pressure was low. It didn't make sense that the engine had stalled out.

Damn him for hurrying his safety checks before taking the craft up. He must have missed something. He must have been so intent on not letting Lindsey go up with him, so scared for his dad, that he'd cut corners. Corners that might mean their lives.

Bart shook his head. He couldn't think of that now. There would be plenty of time to blame himself later. As long as he got them safely to the ground, he could wallow in self-blame the rest of his life, if he chose. Now he needed to focus. He needed to remember everything he'd learned in helicopter flight training or blame wouldn't matter. They would be dead.

Although he'd read about autorotation landings and practiced them on a simulator, he'd never had to perform one for real. And with the stakes so high, he didn't have room for error.

He could feel Lindsey's eyes on him, as wide as the horizon. He wouldn't let her down. He couldn't. He had to think. He had to focus. He had to make sure they survived.

The first order of business was to use the airflow to keep the blades turning. If the blade slowed much more, they'd plummet to the earth like a stone. He reduced the pitch further. The craft inclined forward, the changing airflow powering the blades, speeding the rotation.

So far, so good. Now to bring the craft down.

He established a glide at fifty-five knots. He could hear the rotor spinning slightly faster than it had in powered flight, and as steady as his best ranch horse. The craft began its descent, approaching the ground at an angle of twenty degrees.

The ground loomed closer. The river wound to the side of them, its banks thick with mesquite. A little farther and he could have set down on the grassy plateau. A nice, clear landing. No such luck. It was mesquite tangles or nothing.

He had to reduce airspeed and rate of descent just before touchdown if he wanted to cushion the landing. He moved the cyclic to the rear. The helicopter tipped back slightly, increasing the wind hitting the bottom side of the blades. He applied collective pitch with the pedals. The ground came up fast. He felt Lindsey tense beside him just before the skids hit mesquite.

The copter jolted and bucked. Bart plunged forward.

The harness kept him pinned to the seat with the force of a punch to the sternum. He battled for breath.

The helicopter settled back on its haunches.

And tipped to the side.

The ground came up to meet Bart. The binoculars and something else flew through the air and smacked him in the jaw. Mesquite punched through the side window, stabbing inches from his face. Finally the craft swayed and settled.

Hanging in his belt, Bart struggled to clear his mind. He looked up at Lindsey, suspended above him. Eyes wide, she gripped the harness fastening her to the seat with frantic fingers, knuckles white. She gasped, chest heaving.

"You okay?"

"I think so," she coughed out.

Bart nearly groaned with relief. At least she hadn't been hurt. Shaken up, yes, but she'd recover. Now he just had to figure out a way to get them out of this mess. He grasped the radio. At least they could call for help. Help for them and help for his dad. He flipped on the switch.

The radio was dead.

"Damn."

"Did it break in the landing?"

"I doubt it." Their landing had been rough, but not that rough.

"Then what's wrong with it?"

He groped under the radio, feeling the wires. One hung loose. He pulled it out and looked at the abrupt end.

Lindsey's eyes flared. "It was cut."

"It sure as hell was. And I'll be willing to bet the engine was sabotaged, too."

"Sabotaged," Lindsey whispered under her breath, as if she couldn't quite believe it.

Bart shook his head. He couldn't believe it, either. Despite the vandalism to Lindsey's car and the break-in at her apartment, no one had tried anything this serious. No one had tried to kill them.

Until now.

"Whoever stranded my daddy out on the range probably knew I'd take the helicopter to look for him." Anger constricted his throat like a noose.

"And he sabotaged the engine to make sure you wouldn't return," Lindsey finished. "We have to reach the sheriff's department."

"The ELT should do that for us."

"The ELT?"

"Emergency Location Transmitter. It notifies the authorities when a craft goes down." He groped the spot where the little box was located. His hand grasped air. Another surge of adrenaline dumped into his bloodstream. "The only problem is that it's not here."

"He took it out?"

He nodded. "So when we went down, no one would know where we were." His head pounded. He squinted up at the sky. The clouds were growing thicker by the second. The air was charged with electricity. "We have to find Daddy."

"I have my cell phone. We'll use it to call for

help." She groped around her seat. "If I can find it, that is."

"I think it flew past my face when we tipped." Bart peered into the tangle of mesquite pushing its way up through shards of glass. Sure enough, something small and silver glinted through the gnarled branches. "I see it."

"Can you reach it?"

He tried to fit his hand through broken glass and sharp branches. The phone rested a good four feet below. He couldn't move his hand more than four inches through the shattered window. It was no use. "This damn mesquite is too thick. We're on our own."

Lindsey pushed out a breath of air. But instead of giving in to the fear furrowing her brow and turning her skin to chalk, she raised her chin and met his eyes. "Okay. Let's get out of here and find your father."

"Can you open the door?"

"I think so." She yanked up on the release and pushed. The door opened an inch before gravity slammed it shut again. Gritting her teeth, Lindsey didn't waste a breath before trying again. She pushed harder, this time catching the door with a foot before it closed. She slipped her fingers through the open crack and grabbed the doorframe. "Release my belt."

"Are you sure you can—"

"Release my belt," she repeated.

He did as she asked, using one hand to free her and the other to help support her weight.

She shoved upward. The door flung wide and rested fully open on its hinges.

Bart grasped her waist with both hands, his fingers nearly circling her slender body. "I'll give you a boost. On three."

"Ready."

"One...two...three." He boosted her upward, through the door.

She grasped the skid and pulled herself onto the helicopter's side.

The craft tipped slightly on the scrub and then stilled. Bart released his own harness and scrambled so he was sitting upright in the tight space. He looked up where Lindsey was peering down at him, reaching her hand down to help. "Jump free of the chopper."

"Can you get out by yourself?"

"Yes. Just get free. This thing might tip when I climb out. The last thing we need is for you to get pinned underneath."

She nodded. Lowering herself over the skid, she disappeared from his sight.

The copter swayed on the unstable bed of mesquite. Bart held his breath, afraid to move a muscle. One shift in weight and the thing would roll.

"All clear." Lindsey's voice drifted over the humid wind.

Scooping in a breath, Bart stood and grabbed the edges of Lindsey's door. Pushing off with his legs, he pulled himself out. The craft tipped under his feet. He leaped into the bramble just as the helicopter rolled onto its blades.

A hand closed around his arm before he could pull

himself free of gnarled branches. ''Bart. Are you all right?''

He looked into eyes bluer than Texas bluebells and scrambled to his feet. ''Fine.'' He tried not to look at the helicopter lying nearly belly up beside him.

''Thank God we're safe.''

''Thank God.'' He looked up. The sky overhead was darker, the air oppressive with humidity and alive with electric charge. After checking the ground around the helicopter in vain to see if the change in position would make it possible to reclaim Lindsey's cell phone, he focused on the storm. ''We've got to find Daddy.''

Lindsey squinted up at the clouds. ''Maybe we can get him to some kind of shelter before the storm hits. Do you remember which direction he was heading?''

Before he could answer, a bolt of lightning split the air. Thunder crashed over their heads.

He'd gotten them to the ground, but they were far from safe. And somewhere out in the storm, his dad wandered alone.

RAIN PELTED Lindsey's face. Lightning split the sky, followed by bone-rattling crashes of thunder. She held up a hand, trying to block the raindrops' sting, trying to see through the deluge. It was little use. She could hardly make out Bart, and he was holding her other hand.

''Daddy could be within spitting range and we wouldn't see him,'' Bart said, echoing her thoughts. Rain collected in the brim of his hat and cascaded

down his back in a waterfall. "And this damn lightning is dangerous. We need to find shelter. Wait this
out."

"And leave your father out in this?" she yelled
above the wind.

"Covering this ground isn't going to do a speck of
good if we can't see him."

She knew what he said made sense. It was impossible to see. And the lightning was dangerous. But
still, she couldn't block the memory of Bart's eyes
when he realized his father was a target. His pain at
the thought of losing him. His determination to make
sure that didn't happen. She wouldn't let Bart quit
now. Not when she suspected he wanted to find shelter
for her sake. "If it was just you out here, you'd keep
searching, wouldn't you?"

Bart's brow hardened into a frown.

Answer enough. "We keep looking." Gripping his
hand like a lifeline, she stumbled on.

At first the dark shape on the riverbank looked more
like a heap of clothing than a human being. She picked
up her pace. As they drew closer, she caught a glimpse
of a face and wet gray hair. "Bart!" Lindsey yelled,
pointing.

Bart's head snapped around. He followed her gaze,
his eyes growing wide. Releasing Lindsey's hand, he
sprang into a run.

Hiriam Rawlins lay curled on his side. His arms
were wrapped around his head as if he was protecting
himself from blows. His knees were drawn up to his
chest. And his whole body was shaking.

Reaching the bank, Bart fell to his knees and gathered his father into his arms.

The older man fought against Bart's embrace for a moment. Then his body seemed to relax. His eyes grew less panicked, his face less distraught. Finally he wrapped his arms around his son and lowered his head onto Bart's shoulder. A veined, work-worn hand gently patted Bart's back as if comforting a crying child.

Lindsey stopped in her tracks and watched until tears blurred her vision and mixed with the rain.

LINDSEY FITTED her back into a partially protected hollow in the side of a hill that sloped down to the river. Rain wicked down her hair and dripped from the end of her nose.

Bart lowered himself next to her. Hiriam curled on the other side, his body protected under a shallow shelf of rock. The blanket from the helicopter's first-aid kit wrapped tightly around him, the older man had finally stopped shaking. At least visibly. And at the moment, he appeared to be asleep.

Lindsey couldn't begin to guess all he'd been through today. How he'd gotten so far from the ranch, how frightened and confused he'd been, how cold and miserable and totally alone. How someone could victimize a confused, helpless old man was beyond her. She didn't even want to understand that kind of evil. She shivered and wrapped her arms tight around her middle.

"Here." Bart spread his arms, inviting her inside.

She snuggled against the hard plane of his chest. His arms encircled her. His heat soaked into her. His scent surrounded her and made her feel safe for the first time since the helicopter had gone down.

A miracle.

She thought back to the terror that had claimed her when the helicopter's engine had quit. The cold hand of fear choking her as they had careened to the ground. And the panic that had attacked when Bart pulled out the severed radio wire. "Who would sabotage the helicopter?"

"I have one guess."

"Your cousin." She had only to close her eyes to see Kenny Rawlins glaring at Bart through angry slits as Don read the terms of Jeb's will.

"If both my daddy and I died, Kenny would get his hands not only on the Bar JR, but the Four Aces to boot."

Lindsey nodded. "Would he know how to sabotage a helicopter?"

"He worked as a truck mechanic for a while."

"But that's not the same thing as a helicopter engine, is it?"

"It isn't similar enough for him to know how to *fix* a helicopter engine, but I'll bet it's similar enough to know how to *break* one. And he could take the ELT and cut the radio wires easily enough. It would also be easy for him to get Daddy out of the house unseen. He knows his way around the ranch. He used to live here when he was a kid, before Grandaddy died." Bart's shoulders jerked behind her in a shrug, the movement as tight as a wound spring. "There's only one thing that bothers me."

"What's that?"

"The whole thing seems a bit ambitious for Kenny."

"Working on a helicopter engine?"

"Figuring out who inherits, setting me up for Jeb's murder, the whole thing. He's always stuck to scams that don't require much planning or imagination. The thought of him pulling off something this complicated..." He shook his head. "I just don't know if he's capable. He has to be working with someone."

She had to agree. In the few times she'd met Kenny, she hadn't walked away impressed by his cunning. She searched her mind for possibilities and came up empty. "But it doesn't seem to be Brandy Carmichael. So who?"

"A damn good question."

The thought of one person out there who wanted them out of the way was scary enough. The prospect of two gave her chills. Not that she needed help with those. The rain and wind were doing a fine job. She snuggled against Bart's warmth.

He pulled her closer. "You were something today."

"Me?" She twisted in his arms to look up at him.

He gave her a half smile. "Yes, you. You didn't have to come with me in the helicopter. Hell, I shouldn't have let you."

"That's not your fault. I forced the issue."

"That's what I mean. And after the crash. Most people wouldn't have trudged through the rain looking for my daddy. Not with all that lightning. You never gave up. You never quit. No matter how scared you were, no matter how bad things looked, you wouldn't quit until we found him.''

"Why would I quit?"

His smile grew wider. "Exactly. It doesn't even occur to you to quit. Not everyone is like that. In my experience there are damn few people like that."

She shook her head. "You were the one who was amazing. I had no idea a helicopter could still fly after the engine quit running. I thought we were goners."

"You could have fooled me. I'd say you willed me to land that chopper. Have you always stuck to your guns like that?"

Had she? She had to admit she didn't have any memories of throwing in the towel. Not over anything. A fact that no doubt had caused her parents more than a few headaches. "I suppose I have been pretty tenacious."

"I bet it served you well in law school."

She had to nod. "And with my family."

"Your family?"

"They're a little overprotective." She paused. "Well, a lot overprotective. That's why I moved to Mustang Valley. If I'd stayed in Massachusetts, they'd have built my career for me. I wanted to do it on my own."

"They sound like good people."

She drew in a deep breath. "The greatest," she admitted. "But sometimes they want to do too much. They don't believe I can take care of myself."

Bart nodded as if he'd just figured something out. "That's why you jump down my throat every time I try to help you. Or protect you."

Did she? Yes, she supposed she did. "I can take care of myself. No one seems to believe that."

"I suppose you have brothers."

"Four. All older."

"Ah, I see," he said, as if that explained it all. "So along with planning your career for you, did they follow you around when you went on dates?"

"I didn't go on dates."

"A woman as pretty as you? I can't believe that." He craned his neck to look into her eyes.

Her cheeks heated. She felt as awkward talking about this with Bart as she did with Cara and Kelly. No, *more* awkward. Much more. Bart made her wish she had gone on more dates. He made her wish she had more experience with men. Maybe then she'd know how to handle the feelings kindling inside her.

She took a deep breath. "I come from a family of lawyers. My father is a judge on the Massachusetts Supreme Court, three of my brothers have founded a successful legal firm and the fourth is a federal prosecutor."

"Don't tell me, they chased potential boyfriends away by threatening them with lawsuits."

A chuckle bubbled from her throat. "I wouldn't put it past them. But no, they usually behaved."

"In that case, I can't see any reason those Yankee boys wouldn't be knocking your door down. But then, I've never truly understood Yankees."

She almost shook her head. Bart was something, all right. She'd never been affected by flattery before. But with Bart, the flattery didn't seem like empty words. He made her feel as if every word from his lips had come straight from his heart. "It wasn't the Yankee boys, it was me. I wanted to focus on law school and establishing a legal practice. So I've never had a serious relationship. I've never—" She shook her head. This wasn't coming out right. "Dating was never as important to me as the law." Until now, looking into Bart's eyes. Until now, when she had no business thinking about dating.

"Then it's true." Bart grinned, a teasing glitter to his green eyes. "They really do force you to cut your heart out of your chest as soon as you pass the bar."

Another laugh broke free. It was amazing that Bart still had a sense of humor after all that had happened the past few days and the pressure they were under now. But then, there were so many amazing things about Bart Rawlins, she'd lost count. "I don't want to have to trade my career for a family, that's all."

"Don't you want a family? Don't you want children?" He sounded shocked, as if he couldn't envision that kind of life.

Of course he probably couldn't. Family was what drove Bart. She had only to think of the row of bedrooms he'd planned to fill, of his tenderness when he gathered his father into his arms on the riverbank or of the ache in his eyes when he talked of his mother's death to know that. "Family is important to you, isn't it?"

"It's the most important."

She angled her body so she could look straight into his eyes. "So why aren't you married? Why don't you have children of your own?"

"I haven't found the right woman. With my daddy's illness and my mama…" Regret flickered briefly in his eyes. Then it was gone. He shrugged. "I haven't had a lot of chances to date. Not the last few years anyway."

"You've sacrificed a lot for your parents, haven't you?"

"Sacrifice?" He shook his head. "I wouldn't put it that way. Giving up things isn't sacrifice when you do it for someone you love."

"That sounds like something my mother would say."

"A smart woman. You must take after her."

A chill worked over her skin. She hoped not. She'd been working hard all her adult life not to take after her mother. "My mother is a wonderful woman. A brilliant woman."

"But?"

"But she and I don't see things the same way."

Bart crooked an eyebrow, but he didn't ask. He merely waited for her to go on.

Lindsey drew in a deep breath. "She was a star student at Harvard Law School when she met my dad. They had a real whirlwind love affair and ended up getting married at the end of her second year. By the time the fall semester rolled around, my dad was clerking for a Supreme Court justice and my mom was pregnant with my oldest brother. It wasn't until recently that she finished school and fulfilled her dream of teaching.''

''And you figured if you didn't date, that would never happen to you.''

''It's not that I don't want a family. I do. But I want to establish my career first. I don't want to grow to resent my husband and family, to blame them for my failure to do what I needed to do with my life.''

''Is that how your mother feels about the delay in her career? Does she resent you?''

''No. But I would feel that way. I know I would. The law is too important to me. Proving myself is too important. When I find the right man, when I decide to start a family, I want to be able to give myself without reservation.''

Bart nodded and looked into the darkness. Silence stretched between them, whipped by wind and rain. Finally he returned his gaze to hers, green drilling into blue. ''And you're not afraid of never finding that special person? Of never having a family? Of being alone?'' Deep and ragged, his voice ached with his own misgivings and penetrated a tender spot at the center of her heart.

She swallowed hard. ''I'm scared to death.'' She'd never admitted that before. Not to her family. Not to Kelly and Cara. Not even to herself. She'd spent so much time and energy focused on her career, on proving herself, she'd never realized how much she wanted a man to love her, too. And how afraid she was that she'd have to choose between a man and her career.

She suddenly felt as exposed as a raw nerve. She dipped her head and studied the muddy earth.

He reached out and touched a rough finger to her chin. He tilted her head back so she had to meet his eyes. "A woman like you, there's no reason you shouldn't have it all. The career you want, a husband who dotes on you and children as beautiful as you are."

Warmth bloomed in her cheeks and spread down through her body, radiating from his touch.

"You're one brave woman, Lindsey Wellington. Not many people even know what they want. Even fewer would risk moving halfway across the country on their own to get it."

She didn't feel brave. Not right now. She felt unsure and scared and, oh, so alive. She wanted him to kiss her again. To touch her. To make her feel like he had in her apartment that night—safe and wanted and as if she was facing incredible danger all at the same time. She parted her lips.

His eyes focused on her mouth. "I wish I could kiss you again." He traced a finger along her jaw and over her lower lip. "I wish I could make love to you."

She pursed her lips and kissed his finger.

His eyes seemed to darken. For a moment she thought he'd lower his head and claim her. Instead, he looked away. "The man who makes love to you for the first time should be able to promise you a future. I'm not going to make promises I can't keep."

A chill claimed her, colder than the rain pelting her face. She could reassure him that he'd be acquitted.

She could try to convince him that she needed him far more than she needed any promise. But any argument she made would just be words. And right now they were beyond words.

She laid her head on his shoulder and breathed in his scent. She'd find a way to keep Bart from going to prison for a murder he didn't commit. She had to. The alternative was too tragic to contemplate.

WHEN THE STORM finally let up, armed only with the Maglite they retrieved from the helicopter, they climbed out of the protective hollow and trudged across the rolling land. It was slow going. On a good day, his daddy's arthritis didn't allow him to move very quickly. But now, exhausted from his ordeal, he was moving slower than a show horse's jog. Dawn was bathing the countryside in its gold glow by the time they reached the dirt road stretching from the Four Aces to the highway heading for Mustang Valley.

Bart paused to get a better hold on his dad before turning in the direction of the highway.

Lindsey propped up Daddy's far side. She nodded back in the other direction. "Isn't that the way to the ranch? Or am I all turned around?"

Bart shook his head. He was the one turned around. But not about the direction. The need to pull Lindsey into his arms, to kiss her, to make love to her had pounded through his bloodstream all night long. Even now walking alongside her, watching her face screwed up with concentration from supporting his dad's weight, her little pink tongue darting between her lips every two strides, all he could think about was fitting his mouth over hers and tasting her again.

He surveyed the road ahead. "The highway leading to Mustang Valley is closer. I'm hoping we can flag down a truck to take us to Granbury."

"To the medical center?"

"That's right. Daddy needs a hospital."

As if to illustrate just how badly he needed medical attention, his dad sagged against him. Bart slipped his arms under his back and legs and scooped him into his arms, cradling him like a baby. His dad used to be strapping strong as any cowboy in the area. But though he wasn't two inches shorter than Bart, after nearly ten years of illness he had all the substance of a flake of hay.

Bart picked up his pace. He had to get help. His dad's health was fragile as it was, and a day of wandering the riverbed and a night of huddling out in a thunderstorm and trudging halfway across the ranch hadn't done a speck of good.

By the time they reached the paved highway, Bart's arms had begun to complain about his dad's weight, as unsubstantial as it was. They walked on the gravel shoulder for a good mile before an old blue pickup complete with a loaded gun rack finally rattled toward them. Lindsey stepped out into the road and waved her arms.

The pickup slowed and pulled to the side of the road.

A grizzled man who looked like he was on the north side of sixty and had had a hard life peered out the dusty window. He smiled around a giant plug of chew tucked in one lined cheek.

Lindsey pulled the truck door open. "Thank God you stopped."

"What can I do you for? Need a ride?"

"We need to get to Granbury," Bart said. "To a hospital."

He eyed Bart and his daddy, as if he'd just noticed them. "I see that. Well, what are you waiting for? Pile in."

Lindsey opened the back door of the King Cab. Bart ducked inside, propped his dad gently on the seat and climbed in beside him. Lindsey closed the door and let herself into the front seat.

Obviously damn pleased with the seating arrangement, the man's smile grew wider, highlighting spectacularly stained teeth. He ground the truck into gear and pulled out. "Shep. Shep Davis is the name. So where are you folks from?"

"The Four Aces," Lindsey answered. "Our helicopter broke down out on the range."

"Had to pull an emergency landing, huh?"

Lindsey smiled and glanced back at him. "Bart landed it like the pro he is."

Bart tensed. Watching the man's face in the rearview mirror, he waited for him to link the Four Aces with the name Bart. After that it would only be a short skip to realizing he had a suspected murderer riding in his truck. If they were lucky, he might just toss them out on the side of the road. If not, Bart could very well find the barrel of one of those shotguns pointed in his face.

The guy behind the wheel just smiled at Lindsey as if the two of them were the only ones in the truck. "If you ask me, helicopters are ruining ranching. So loud and damn expensive. They scare the cattle and bankrupt the rancher."

Bart bit his tongue. He hadn't liked the idea of the helicopter, either. But the fact was, qualified cowboys were hard to find these days. It took years of experience to make a hand. Kids nowadays were more interested in learning to toss a football so they could be the next Troy Aikman than learning to rope cattle. Adding the helicopter to help out the horses and cowboys had saved the Four Aces from the labor problems that had devastated many other ranches in the area.

"Are you a rancher?" Lindsey tilted her head toward Shep, as if truly interested.

An unmistakable pang shot through Bart and settled in his chest. How could he be jealous of a sixty-year-old coot who had half a can of tobacco bulging from one cheek? It was ridiculous. Especially when he should be glad Lindsey was distracting the man and keeping him from adding one and one and tossing them out on the side of the road before they reached Granbury.

He concentrated on his dad's shallow breathing and tried to ignore the small talk in the front seat.

"I ain't a rancher. Not anymore. Used to work on one out here, though. The Bar JR."

Bart's ears pricked up. So much for his attempt at ignoring their conversation.

Lindsey nodded and glanced into the back seat. "The Bar JR? That's Jeb Rawlins's ranch."

"That's the one."

"How long ago did you work there?"

"A good twenty years ago. Old bastard quit paying me and stole my woman. By the time I moved down to Waco, I'd lost four months' wages and gained a broken heart."

"That's terrible." Lindsey's voice rang with sympathy. "Do you still live in Waco?"

"Nope, just moved back."

"I see."

Bart could see she was planning to fish for information on Jeb. Anything that would point to someone else as the murderer. And old Shep's financial ruin and jealousy made good motives. Bart just hoped her prying didn't refresh Shep's memory and help him connect the dots. His dad would likely recover now with a little patching up and rest, but if they had to walk from here to Granbury, things wouldn't be so rosy.

Up in the front seat, Lindsey's strategy was working. Shep nodded, his head jiggling up and down like one of those bobblehead dolls. He spat out the open window before turning bright eyes back to Lindsey, obviously eager to share his life's story with his beautiful audience. "I guess now that Jeb's dead, I won't see a dime. Shame. With the economy the way it is, I could use the bucks. I suppose I'll sue the estate, but

I don't expect that'll do me a hell of a lot of good. You can't get blood from a stone.''

Bart nearly groaned. It looked like the Bar JR was turning into exactly what Jeb intended it to be: a black hole that would suck money from the Four Aces. Jeb's revenge.

Shep narrowed his eyes on Lindsey. ''Know any honest lawyers?''

''Actually, yes. I'm with Lambert & Church in Mustang Valley.''

''You're a lawyer? No kidding?''

''No kidding.'' Lindsey smiled and then stared at him with rapt fascination. ''What about the woman you loved? Tell me about her.''

''Beatrice? It didn't last with her and Jeb. At least that's what I heard.''

A bad feeling crept up Bart's spine. ''Beatrice? Not Beatrice Jensen.''

The grizzled face peered at him from the rearview mirror. ''You know her?''

Bart paused, not wanting to answer.

''What am I thinking? Of course you know her. She works at the Four Aces now, doesn't she?'' The lines in his brow grew deeper. ''What did you say your name was?''

Oh, hell. Hearing Beatrice's name in connection to Jeb's had surprised him so much, he'd plumb forgot to keep his damn mouth shut.

Shep adjusted the mirror so he could get a good look at Bart's face. ''You're Bart Rawlins, ain't ya?''

Bart gave Shep a reluctant nod.

Shep turned in Lindsey's direction. "And I'll bet that makes you the lawyer who's fixing to get him off on those murder charges."

"Bart didn't kill his uncle, Mr. Davis. He's innocent."

"I thought I told you to call me Shep. Even my daddy was never Mr. Davis." He turned back to Bart, his eyes hardening. "And I don't care what you did to Jeb. He deserved what he got. But by pulling that knife on him, you took away any chance I had to get my money."

Bart held up a hand. "You make sure we get to the medical center in Granbury, and I'll see you get your money."

"You're serious?"

Bart nodded. "And on the way, you tell us everything you know about Beatrice Jensen."

Chapter Eleven

Lindsey accepted the steaming cup of bitter-smelling coffee Bart handed her and watched him sink into the hospital waiting-room chair next to her. Fortunately his promise of money had convinced Shep Davis to bring them to the Lake Granbury Medical Center and now Bart's father was getting the medical attention he needed. Unfortunately, Shep hadn't been able to tell them much about Beatrice that Bart didn't already know—at least not about the present-day Beatrice. After Jeb stole her affections, Shep had had little to do with the woman.

Lindsey peered at Bart over her cup. Her mind had been whirring since Shep had told them his story. "What if we've been thinking about Jeb's murder the wrong way? What if the motives involved are entirely different from what we've assumed?"

"You mean, what if he wasn't killed for his land?"

"That's exactly what I mean. What if there's some other motive behind his murder? A motive like jealousy?"

"You're thinking of Beatrice."

"Could she still be in love with Jeb?"

"Maybe. I don't know. Before today, I didn't have a clue they even knew each other. And now she's missing. Very suspicious." He frowned, his eyebrows pulling low over green eyes. "But isn't a murder due to jealousy usually done in a fit of passion? Beatrice finds out Jeb's been running around and confronts him with a knife? That kind of thing? Whoever killed Jeb had to do some fancy planning in advance or they couldn't have framed me."

Lindsey pursed her lips in thought. He had a point. "Maybe she didn't kill Jeb. But she could have left your father out on the range to lash back at you for Jeb's murder."

"It would explain how Daddy got out of the house without anyone at the ranch seeing him. But it doesn't explain the helicopter."

"Kenny?"

"Gary said he was at the ranch. But I can't think of one reason Beatrice would work with Kenny."

"Mr. Rawlins?" a deep voice said.

Lindsey looked in the direction of the voice. A rough-hewn man with black hair and skin the color of a copper penny peered down at Bart. "I'm Dr. Mendoza. I've just examined your father."

Bart sprang to his feet.

Lindsey rose beside him and placed a supportive hand on his arm.

He glanced at her, giving her a grateful smile.

Warmth curled through her. It must have been so hard for him, facing his father's illness alone, facing his mother's death alone. She was glad she could offer some comfort. Some support. Pulling in a deep breath, Bart looked back to the doctor. "How is he?"

"He's doing amazingly well under the circumstances."

"When can he come home?"

The doctor held up a hand. "Not so fast. I said he was doing well *under the circumstances,* not that he was ready to go back to life as usual."

Bart tensed. "Spit it out, Doc."

"He needs to stay here for a while. Maybe a few days. After that, I suggest he goes to a rehabilitation center. He's going to need around-the-clock skilled care for a while."

Hospital. Rehabilitation center. Skilled care. Lindsey's head spun at the possible implications. Bart's father was in worse shape than she'd realized.

Beside her, Bart clenched his teeth. "Whatever my daddy needs to get better, he'll get." His voice was clipped, harsh, as if he was having trouble controlling his anger. Anger no doubt directed at the person who was responsible for his father's condition.

"We should know more in the next couple days," the doctor said.

"Can Bart see him?" Lindsey asked. "Before we leave?"

"Certainly."

"And Doc?" Bart said. "No one is allowed in my daddy's room besides the two of us and any medical staff that needs to see him. No one. Not friends and certainly not family. I've called an outside security firm to watch over him. They should be here within the hour.''

The doctor hesitated for a moment and then nodded. ''Whatever you wish, Mr. Rawlins.'' After exchanging thank-yous and goodbyes, the doctor left.

Once they were alone, Lindsey looked up at Bart, searching his eyes. She could feel anger pulsing off him in waves. Anger born from worry for his father and frustration at not having been able to protect him. But even though she understood where his anger was coming from, it concerned her just the same. ''We'll find out who did this, Bart. And we'll make sure your father isn't hurt again.''

Bart gave a sharp nod. ''Damn straight we will. But before anything else happens, I need to talk to the sheriff first, and then Don Church.''

''Don Church? About Jeb's will?''

''About changing my own.''

''LINDSEY, BART, where have you been? I've been trying to reach both of you since yesterday.''

Bart and Lindsey strode past Nancy Wilks and straight down the hall to Don's office. There was no time to stop and chat. He had to see Don. Kenny or Beatrice or whoever the hell was behind what had happened to his dad weren't going to get away with what they'd done. Not if he had anything to say about it. And although things weren't as clear-cut as they'd seemed when Kenny appeared to be the only one who would profit by Jeb's death, Bart's money was still on his cousin. Money he was going to make damn sure Kenny never got his hands on.

Beside him, Lindsey glanced at Nancy as she walked. "Nancy, we need to see Don," she explained. "It's urgent."

"You need to listen to your voice mail. The grand jury came back with a true bill. Bart's arraignment is scheduled for tomorrow."

Bart nearly stumbled. He knew the chances were nearly one hundred percent that the grand jury would vote to indict. Lindsey had explained to him that a grand jury rarely acted as more than a rubber stamp for the prosecution. And in Bart's case, the district attorney had far too much evidence for any grand jury to ignore, even if they wanted to.

Lindsey gave him a worried glance but kept on walking. They rounded the corner and reached Don's office. The door stood open. No one was inside.

Lindsey whirled to face Nancy. "Where's Don?"

"Paul's office."

Lindsey met Bart's eyes, and the two of them started back in the direction of Paul's office.

"Wait!" Nancy scampered to keep up with them, her breath labored. "Paul and Don are in a meeting."

They reached Paul's closed door. Lindsey planted her feet in the hallway. "So we'll wait. We need to talk to Don right away."

"Suit yourself." Nancy eyed Lindsey and bobbed her head. "What happened to you?"

Lindsey looked down at her wrinkled suit and

nearly shredded stockings as if she hadn't realized how she looked until this minute.

Bart cringed. In his urgency to find out who was responsible for his father's condition, he'd forgotten they'd spent the past twenty-four hours searching through mesquite in a thunderstorm and hiking halfway across Texas. "I'm sorry, Lindsey. I didn't even think of giving you a chance to clean up. Do you want to stop back at the ranch before we talk to Don?"

She smoothed a hand over her hair and raised her chin, a dignified expression gracing her face. "This is more important than appearances."

Just as he opened his mouth to tell her she didn't have to worry about appearances, that she always looked great, the mahogany door swung wide and Paul Lambert stood in the doorway.

Surprise registered in his face. His gaze traveled from Lindsey's drip-dried hair to the mud clinging to Bart's boots. "Lindsey, Bart, what happened?"

"We need to talk to Don," Lindsey said.

A young man, his hair the color of coffee with too much cream, stepped up beside Paul and leveled beaming brown eyes on Lindsey.

The surprised look still on Paul's face, he glanced at his client. "Roger Rosales, I'd like you to meet Bart Rawlins and Lindsey Wellington."

Rosales gave them a practiced smile. "Nice to meet you."

"Lindsey is a lawyer here at the firm and Bart is one of our best clients," Paul continued.

Ignoring Bart, Rosales horned in on Lindsey. "Wellington. Not one of the Boston Wellingtons?"

Lindsey nodded stiffly. "How do you know my family, Mr. Rosales?"

"It's Roger. My company has holdings in the Boston area."

"Your company?"

"Ranger Corporation. I'm in charge of regional development, so I'm based in this area. But I have occasion to travel to Boston."

Bart had heard of Ranger Corporation. Who hadn't? The company was huge, with its fingers in pies all over the world.

Lindsey looked down at her wrinkled suit. A flush of embarrassment stained her cheeks. "Please excuse my appearance. It's been a tough day."

"I hope it improves."

"So do I." She glanced past Rosales and Paul to where Don stood in the back of the office. "It was nice meeting you."

"Thank you. Meeting you has been an unexpected perk." He gave her a beaming grin.

Bart stiffened. He didn't like Roger Rosales, and it wasn't hard to figure out why. The man was too good-looking, too charming, and the interest in his eyes when he looked at Lindsey made Bart want to clock him.

"Paul, Don…" Roger said. "I trust you'll get in touch with me."

Paul stuck out his hand and shook Roger's. "We

sure will.'' Don gave a wave and a nod from across the room. As soon as the Ranger Corporation executive disappeared down the hall, Paul zeroed in on Lindsey. ''Okay, what happened?'' His voice was sharp with obvious concern.

Bart stepped closer to Lindsey. ''Someone tried to kill us and my daddy. We're here to make sure it doesn't happen again.''

''Tried to kill you?'' Paul looked to Nancy, still hovering behind Bart and Lindsey. ''Call Ben.''

Bart turned to Nancy and held up a hand. ''We already talked to him at the hospital.''

''Hospital?'' Paul repeated.

''My daddy is in rough shape.''

''I'm sorry. I hope he'll be okay.''

Joining them at the door, Don added his concern to Paul's. ''So how can we help?''

''I need to change my will.''

''What would changing your will…'' Don trailed off, understanding dawning on his face. ''You think Kenny did this. That he tried to kill you and your father so he can inherit both the Bar JR and the Four Aces.''

''Damn straight. And the best way to keep that from happening is changing my will and my daddy's will so the son of a bitch won't get a single square foot of land.''

Don nodded. ''We can do that. Since you hold power of attorney, it won't be a problem. We'll set up a trust for your father, and stipulate that upon his death the holdings go to charity or wherever you'd like. Are you still planning to sell the Four Aces if…''

Bart let out a breath. Don didn't have to say the word *convicted* for Bart to know what he was getting at. ''I suppose I am. I don't have much of a choice.''

Don turned to Paul. ''Do you want to make sure the paperwork is ready, just in case?''

Lindsey shook her head adamantly. ''We won't have to go that far. Bart isn't going to be convicted.'' She stood with her chin raised, her spine straight as a fence post and the fire of an avenging angel burning in her eyes. Like she was ready to fight by his side to the end.

An uneasy feeling niggled at the back of his mind.

''You're right, Lindsey. He won't have to worry about selling the ranch. He's going to be acquitted,'' Paul said. He frowned at Don. ''In the meantime, didn't you have another problem you wanted to discuss with Bart?''

Another problem. Bart almost cringed. He focused on Don. ''What is it?''

''Someone is contesting Jeb's will.''

Now it was Bart's turn to stare in surprise. ''Not Kenny?''

''No, not Kenny.''

Of course not. No one who knew the Bar JR's financial state would want the ranch. No one without a family legacy to protect at any rate. ''Then who?''

Don shifted his feet on the thick carpet, as if he didn't want to answer.

''Who, Don?''

The portly lawyer sighed and looked at the floor. "Beatrice. Beatrice Jensen. She claims she married Jeb twenty years ago."

BOOTS THUMPING down the hallway of the ranch house, Bart headed straight for Beatrice's living quarters, Lindsey right behind him. His dad's nurse had a heap of explaining to do. He didn't care that she was contesting Jeb's will. Even though he'd love to reunite the original Rawlins ranch, he'd never expected to inherit the Bar JR in the first place. But the news that she'd been Jeb's estranged wife for the past twenty years and never told him had flattened him like a well-aimed fist.

He pounded a fist on Beatrice's door. "Beatrice? We need to talk."

Nothing answered him but the soft sounds of his and Lindsey's breathing.

He knocked again.

Still nothing.

"Damn." He grasped the knob. It turned easily under his hand. Pushing open the door, he flipped on the light.

The room was as barren as the day before Beatrice moved in. No clutter in the bathroom, no sheets on the bed, no sign a human lived here at all.

Lindsey looked up at him. "I guess we didn't have to worry that something bad happened to her. She just filed her claim against Jeb's estate and moved out."

He ran a hand over his face. "I'm glad I hired security for Daddy. If she was the one who left him out on the range…''

''Would any of the hands know where she might have gone?''

''I doubt it, but it's worth asking around.''

They found Gary and some of the hands in one of the corrals. Covered with dust, Gary's bay mare was dark with sweat. Foam lathered where the reins touched her neck. ''How's your daddy doing, Bart?'' Gary said, looking from Bart to Lindsey.

''He's going to be in the hospital for a while. I'll let you know when he can have visitors.''

Gary nodded. ''Got word that the FAA is sending someone out to investigate the helicopter crash. You call them?''

''I imagine Sheriff Ben did.'' Bart was glad the FAA would investigate. At least he wouldn't have to rely on Hurley Zeller to get to the bottom of the helicopter sabotage.

''How about Beatrice? The sheriff find her?'' Gary asked.

The sheriff. What a joke. Bart didn't even know if the sheriff had searched. ''Looks like Beatrice moved out on her own. Any of you know anything about it?''

''Can't say I do.'' Gary glanced at the cowboys riding behind him. ''You boys?''

A chorus of nopes and shaking heads answered.

''Anyone see her yesterday?'' Bart glanced at the group of faces to the same result.

Gary's brow furrowed. ''You can't be thinking Beatrice sabotaged the helicopter. She wouldn't know a blade from a cyclic.''

"I'm thinking she may have done something to Daddy.''

Gary shook his head. "I can't see it. Beatrice loves that old man.''

That's what Bart had thought, too. Until his daddy's life had been put in danger. Until he'd learned Beatrice was married to Jeb.

Gary grunted. "Unless…''

Bart's pulse picked up its pace. "Unless what?''

"Something Kenny said when I ran him off the ranch yesterday. Made it seem like he was here to see Beatrice.''

A shot of adrenaline slammed into Bart's bloodstream. "Why didn't you mention this yesterday?''

"I didn't believe him when he said it. I thought he was just making up excuses to be here so he could cause trouble.''

Anger throbbed in Bart's ears. But the anger wasn't directed at Gary. It was aimed squarely at Kenny. His cousin wasn't much of a planner, but somehow he'd stumbled on the perfect plan to ruin Bart's life and the lives of everyone he cared about.

And Bart damn well wasn't going to let him get away with it.

LINDSEY COULD SEE the anger work its way from Bart's hat to his boots, tensing every muscle and balling his hands into fists on the way. So when he spun on a heel, she was ready.

She stepped in front of him, blocking his path. "Where are you going?"

"I have to take care of something." He stepped around her without missing a beat. His long legs and rolling stride closed the distance to the truck with remarkable speed.

She ran to catch up. "Tell me you're not going to confront Kenny."

"I should have done it a long damn time ago." He yanked open the door.

Lindsey raced around the truck. She couldn't let Bart rush off like this. If she could keep him talking, maybe he'd calm down and see this confrontation as the mistake it was. Maybe he'd listen to reason. She opened the door and scrambled into the passenger seat.

Bart glanced at her out of the corner of his eye. His lips flattened into a hard line, as if he was unhappy she'd tagged along but not surprised. He slipped the key into the ignition and cranked the engine to life. Shifting the truck into gear, he accelerated down the driveway and out the gate.

Lindsey strapped herself in and held on. "You can't talk to Kenny. Not until you calm down."

He looked straight ahead, eyes hard. A muscle twitched along his jaw.

"This will just lead to a fistfight."

He pulled onto the highway and accelerated.

"Your arraignment is scheduled for tomorrow, Bart. You don't want the kind of headlines another fight between you and Kenny will cause. Not unless you want all of Mustang County to believe you're guilty.

You have to report this to the sheriff, let the law deal with Kenny.''

"The law has done nothing but railroad me for a murder I didn't commit."

She couldn't argue with him there. She could understand his growing cynicism. "Give the system another chance, Bart. You can't take matters into your own hands."

"Can't I? Daddy could have died out on the range. Hell, we may never have found him. And you were in that helicopter. You could have—" He stopped abruptly, as if he couldn't push the words past his lips.

"Your father is doing well, and I'm right here. You have to listen to me."

Bart stared straight ahead as if he hadn't heard a word. Reaching the city limits in record time, he slowed. A couple blocks later, he swung into the parking lot of Hit 'Em Again. The lot was filled with pickup trucks, nearly every one equipped with a gun rack. The windows and doors of the tavern stood open. A steel guitar wailed into the warm evening.

Bart swung the truck into one of the few free spaces, threw open the door and dismounted, slamming the door behind him. Hands hardened into fists, he strode for the tavern.

Lindsey scrambled to catch up. She grasped his hard biceps just as he reached for the door. "Don't do this, Bart. Please."

He looked down at her, his gaze sweeping over her face and zeroing in on her eyes. "Sometimes a man has to stand up, Lindsey, and protect the people he cares about. I can't sit by while Kenny tries to hurt you or Daddy. I wouldn't be much of a man if I did.'' He turned away from her, yanked open the door and strode into the tavern.

A shiver worked over her skin and settled in her chest. *Protect the people he cares about.* He'd included her in that select group. Her and his father.

She caught the door before it swung closed and followed him into the swirl of smoke and country music.

The place was packed. Couples whirled on the dance floor, their cowboy boots moving in the rhythm of a Texas two-step. A band crowded onto a bandstand in the corner. A short, wiry man stood center stage and belted out a heartbreak song in the deepest voice she'd ever heard. Through the smoke, music and laughter, she spotted Kenny. His back to the bar, he tipped a beer and stared through narrowed eyes at the people blowing off steam around him.

Setting his jaw, Bart headed in his cousin's direction.

When Kenny spotted him, he pushed off the bar and stood on boots wobbly from booze. ''You have some nerve, Bart.'' His voice boomed, rising above the music and noise.

Heads snapped around. Curious eyes followed the exchange.

Lindsey cringed. If this confrontation erupted into a fistfight, there would be plenty of witnesses. Just what Bart didn't need.

''I heard you stopped at the Four Aces yesterday, Kenny.''

"The Four Aces? What are you talking about?"

"Don't play dumb with me."

"Dumb? You're the one who's dumb. Coming around me. I ought to grab that shotgun over the bar and put some buckshot in you right now for killing my old man. No one would blame me."

"Stay away from the Four Aces. Stay away from my daddy and Lindsey. I'm warning you."

"Well, thanks for the warning, cousin. I guess that's more than you gave my old man."

"Go to hell, Kenny."

"You planning to send me there like you did my daddy?"

"I didn't kill Jeb. But so help me God, if you do anything to hurt my daddy or Lindsey or the Four Aces again, I will kill you. And I won't need a knife. I'll do it with my bare hands."

Kenny turned to the people around him. "He threatened me. You heard that, didn't you? He said he was going to kill me."

Lindsey closed her eyes and prayed the scene wouldn't come back to haunt them.

Chapter Twelve

Shifting in his seat behind the defendant's table in Mustang Valley Superior Court, Bart watched people file into the courtroom and take seats in the galley behind him. People who by now probably had heard all about his appearance at Hit 'Em Again last night.

He'd been damn stupid. Stupid to confront Kenny and stupider still to threaten to kill him in front of all those people. He should have listened to Lindsey. He should have held his temper.

As if that had been possible.

When he'd heard Kenny was at the ranch visiting Beatrice the day his dad disappeared and the helicopter was sabotaged, he'd lost all sense of reason. Kenny had tried to take from him everything he cared about, *everyone* he cared about.

And hell, he *would* kill his cousin and gladly do the time if it meant keeping his dad and Lindsey safe.

Lindsey.

She leaned forward in the chair next to him studying a legal document. Her hair draped over her shoulder like a silken veil.

He wasn't sure when she had worked her way under his skin. But he couldn't deny that she had. She had the refinement of a true lady, yet the tenacity of a coon dog. And the way she put herself on the line for him, for what she believed in, for all that was right in the world, truly humbled him.

He'd never killed more than a couple of coyotes in all his years, but he wouldn't hesitate to choke the life out of Kenny with his bare hands if that's what it took to protect her and his daddy.

"The Mustang Valley Superior Court is now in session," a bailiff barked out. "The Honorable Judge Enrique Valenzuela presiding. All rise."

Bart glanced back at the gallery. The seats were filled with concerned citizens, retirees with some hours to fill and reporters, not just from Mustang Valley but Dallas/Fort Worth, as well. The owner of the *Mustang Gazette,* crusty old Beau Jennings, peered over his glasses from the back of the room. And beside her boss stood Lindsey's friend, Cara Hamilton. Bart gave Cara a brief nod before turning his attention back to the front of the courtroom.

The distinguished-looking judge swept into the room in black robes and perched on the mahogany bench in front of the American flag and the Lone Star flag of Texas.

Bart stifled a smile. He'd gone to grade school with Enrique Valenzuela, or Rico as he was called in those days. He'd been a smart-mouthed little whelp back then. Who knew he'd grow up to be the youngest and most respected judge in the county. And one of the toughest.

Rico scanned the room through tiny rimless glasses. "We have two arraignments this morning, as I understand it."

The bailiff glanced at the docket. "Yes, Judge."

"Then let's have the first case."

The bailiff announced the name of a cowboy Bart had seen many times at Hit 'Em Again and the charge levied against him. Drunk driving. The cowboy pleaded not guilty. That bit of business dispensed, Rico looked at Bart point-blank and nodded to the bailiff.

Lindsey's hand found his under the table. Her soft fingers wrapped around his and squeezed.

The bailiff seemed to straighten, suddenly formal. "The court calls Bartholomew J. Rawlins."

Releasing his hand, Lindsey rose. Bart pushed to his feet beside her.

The bailiff continued. "In the name and by authority of the State of Texas, the grand jury of Mustang County, State of Texas do present that Bartholomew J. Rawlins in said county and state did commit a criminal homicide of the first degree against the peace and dignity of the State."

Bart had thought he understood the charge he was facing. But hearing it read aloud in such a formal manner shook him to the soles of his Tony Lamas.

The judge focused on Bart. "How do you plead, Bart? Are you guilty or not guilty?"

Bart swallowed into a dry throat. "Not guilty, Your Honor."

Rico nodded. "And you're out on bail, as I understand it."

"Your Honor?" a voice said from the other side of the courtroom.

Bart snapped around to look in the direction of the voice. He hadn't noticed the man sitting at the other table until now. But he knew him. Fifty if he was a day, yet bursting with the energy of a squirrely colt, Marshall Kramer had peppered the county with advertisements while running for the post of District Attorney. Hell, Bart had even voted for the guy.

"Yes, Marshall?" Judge Rico said.

Marshall adjusted his three-piece suit. Where one of Marshall's three assistants had handled the drunk driving case, the charge of murder clearly counted for enough to justify Marshall taking the case himself. "I have some concerns about the defendant's bail."

Next to Bart, Lindsey stiffened. She kept her eyes focused on the judge.

"And what would those concerns be?" Rico asked.

Marshall raised the *Mustang Gazette* with a flourish. The headline blared for all to see—Murder Defendant Makes Threat. "The defendant was overheard threatening one of the witnesses against him last night."

Judge Rico nodded as if he'd already heard the story. With the speed of gossip around Mustang Valley, he probably had. Many times.

Bart inwardly cringed.

"And?" the judge prompted.

"And we would like his bail revoked."

His words cut into Bart like a cold blade.

"Your Honor," Lindsey said in a controlled voice that belied the tension Bart could feel emanating from her. "May I address the court?"

"Go ahead, Ms. Wellington."

"My client was severely provoked to say what he did. If I could show you the mitigating circumstances, I'm sure you'd agree. So I'd like to request we delay this decision pending a hearing."

"I don't think that's necessary, Judge." Marshall looked around the room, like he wanted to pace but couldn't find the acreage. "The defendant said he was going to kill a man. The son of the man he's accused of murdering, no less. I have a dozen witnesses. He's a danger to public safety, and we need to get him off the streets as soon as possible."

Behind him in the gallery, Bart could hear reporters' pens scratching down every word. The blade of impending disaster sunk a little deeper.

"Your Honor," Lindsey said. "Bart is a lifelong resident of Mustang Valley. He's never been charged with anything until now. To assume he's a danger to public safety without a hearing—"

"Point taken, Ms. Wellington. We'll set a hearing date for early next week. That should give both sides a few days to interview the witnesses." He looked down at Bart, his black eyes deadly serious. "And Bart? Use that time to get your affairs in order. If I find that you have indeed been threatening witnesses, you'll find yourself awaiting trial behind bars."

The blade filleted him from breast to belly. He had no doubt what the judge would find. And it was going to be awfully tough to protect Lindsey and his daddy while he was sitting in a jail cell.

LINDSEY SET DOWN her fork for the fifteenth time and watched the shadows in Bart's eyes. By the time they got back to the ranch, evening was closing in on the rolling hills. After she'd helped Bart feed the horses, they'd sequestered themselves in the kitchen to eat and discuss the upcoming hearing. So far they'd done little of either.

She looked down at the macaroni and cheese she'd made, congealing on her plate. She didn't know what she'd been thinking. The simple meal had smoothed over problems when she was a child, but it would take more than comfort food to fix things now. She pushed her plate away nearly untouched and returned her attention to Bart.

He was looking straight at her.

Her stomach gave a little jolt.

"What are you thinking about?"

She glanced at the table, noticing his plate was untouched, as well. "That I should have made something different to eat."

"It's fine. You could have whipped up a gourmet meal and I wouldn't have been able to choke it down. Not after today."

The jolt she'd felt in her stomach turned into a cold lump. Not after today. Today, when a hearing was the best she could come up with to deflect the prosecution's request to revoke bail. A hearing where a parade of witnesses from Hit 'Em Again would get up on the stand and testify that Bart had threatened to kill his cousin.

"Now what are you thinking?" Bart asked again.

She looked into his eyes and forced a confident smile. "I was just thinking of witnesses I could put on the stand at the hearing."

"And coming up empty?"

She opened her mouth to protest, but the words died on her lips. He wouldn't buy any slick answers she gave anyway. "I'm sorry."

"You're the last person who should apologize. If I'd listened to you instead of my hot head, I wouldn't be in this fix." His green eyes were dark, haunted. His rough features were twisted with regret.

She drew in a deep breath. "It's past, done. Now we have to move on, figure out what we can do from here."

"I'll hire a bodyguard for you and beef up security for Daddy. The two of you will be safe. I'll make sure of it, whether I'm here or in jail awaiting trial."

"I don't need a bodyguard because you're not going to jail."

He raised his brows. "How do you figure that? I did just what Marshall said I did. I threatened to kill Kenny."

"We'll show that you did it out of fear for your life, your father's life and my life. That you only did it to make Kenny back off."

"And how do we show that?"

"I'll call Gary. I'll call Brandy Carmichael. Both can tell the court a few things about Kenny's recent conduct."

"And mine. Gary saw how angry I was when I set out to Hit 'Em Again. Brandy saw me throw a punch at Kenny."

He was right. Each of them could testify to a piece of what Kenny had done to Bart, but they could also give damaging testimony. And she had no doubt Marshall would bring out the other side at the hearing. "What about me? I've been part of everything. I've seen what Kenny has done. I know you were just trying to protect us."

"You can be a witness and my attorney at the same time?"

"Well, no. I'd have to step down as your attorney."

"Then we can't do that, either."

"We can find another attorney, Bart. Someone with a lot more experience."

"No. Besides, if you stepped down as my attorney you could also testify to how angry I was that night. And that I threatened to kill Kenny. And coming from you, that's got to carry extra weight with the judge."

He was right about that, too. She blew out a frustrated breath and dropped her chin to her chest. Her hair swung over her shoulders and draped around her face. "I'll think of something. There has to be something."

He leaned forward. Reaching across the corner of the table, he smoothed her hair back from her cheek and tilted her chin up. His touch was so tender, shivers stole down her spine. "There isn't any way around the truth, Lindsey. They're going to revoke my bail. I'm going back to jail." He paused, looking into her eyes with such longing she thought her own heart would break. "I just can't help wishing…" He trailed off, his voice hoarse.

"What? What do you wish?"

He withdrew his hand and rested it on the corner of the table, as if gripping the solid surface for support. "It doesn't matter."

She laid her hand on his. His fingers were rough, the skin thick with calluses. But she could feel a slight tremor run through him at her touch. "It matters. It matters to me."

He raised his eyes to hers. He watched her for a long time, and when he finally spoke, it was in a whisper. "I wish I could look at you across a crowded dance hall and know that you were saving every dance for me."

The tremor traveled up her arm and settled in her chest. "What else do you wish?"

"I wish we could ride bareback together under a moonlit sky."

Her chest tightened. She struggled to breathe. "And?"

"I wish I could show you just how deeply and thoroughly a man can love a woman."

She leaned toward him, wanting the corner of the table between them to disappear, wanting his arms around her, wanting to feel the solidness of his chest pressed against her breasts. She stood and stepped around the table.

He rose beside her. His hands hung at his sides, his fingers flexing and straightening, as if he wanted to touch her but couldn't. "And most of all, I wish we had a future stretching in front of us. A future a thousand miles long and a hundred years deep."

"We have tonight."

He sucked in a breath. "That's not enough."

"It's enough for me. Right now it's all I could ever ask for." She reached out and laid her hands on his chest. She could feel the steady beat of his heart under the crisp white cotton. A heart so strong. A heart so tender. She slid her hands upward until she could clasp them around his neck. Until her own heart pressed against his. Looking deep into his tortured green eyes, she pulled him down to her.

He let her guide him, as if he couldn't mount a fight. But when he claimed her lips, she could tell he wanted this as much as she did.

His lips caressed hers, warm and tender. But there was an urgency underlying the kiss. A desperation. An overwhelming need. A need for her.

And the need within her answered.

He slipped his tongue into her mouth and deepened the kiss.

Warmth rushed through her body, making her light-headed, making her knees weak. She sagged against him.

He pulled her into his strong arms. Breaking the kiss, he narrowed his eyes with unspoken questions.

"Make love with me, Bart. Please," she whispered.

He scooped her into his arms and held her tight against his chest. Boots thunking on wood, he climbed the stairs and carried her to his bedroom.

He didn't switch on the light, but moved into the darkness and set her gently on her feet near the bed. He slid open a drawer in the nightstand and rummaged inside. Producing a book of matches, he struck one and set the flame to the wick of a candle next to the bed.

Light flickered over his face and shone in his blond hair.

She swallowed hard and forced her voice to function. "That's nice."

"I wish I had more. A wall of candles. Music. Flowers. Your first time should be special. Romantic."

"All I need is you. You make it special. Romantic."

He looked away, as if he didn't quite believe her.

She reached up. Grasping the brim of his hat, she lifted it off his head and set in on her own. It settled low on her forehead, nearly covering her eyes.

A small smile curved his lips.

She tilted her head back to peer up at him under the huge hat. "Sexy, huh?"

"You make anything look sexy." He grasped the hat's crown and lifted it off her head. With a flick of his wrist, he tossed it on a chair. Heat in his eyes, he gathered her against him and lowered his mouth to hers once again.

His lips and tongue nipped and played over hers.

Once her mouth had been thoroughly kissed, he moved his lips over her neck to her collarbone.

Heat spiraled through her and centered deep within her body. She wanted to touch him, for him to touch her. She wanted to be closer.

As if reading her mind, he slipped his hands under her suit jacket, under her blouse, until his work-roughened skin scraped along her sides.

She wanted more. She wanted him to touch all of her, see all of her, kiss all of her. She arched her back, pressing against him, savoring the feel of his hands.

He moved his fingers over her ribs. When he reached her bra, he slipped his fingers underneath, pushing it up and out of the way. His hands covered her breasts, cupping, holding.

She sucked in a breath.

His fingers teased her nipples. His tongue and lips took her, devoured her. Finally he pulled his hands from her breasts and found the buttons of her jacket. The jacket hit the floor, followed by her blouse and bra until she stood before him naked from the waist up.

He stood an arm's length from her and drew in a shuddering breath. "Lord, you're beautiful."

Shivers pebbled her skin and raised her nipples to tight nubs. With him looking at her this way, she felt beautiful. She felt loved. She felt powerful. And she wanted more.

She held out her arms, but he didn't step into them. Instead, he peeled off his own shirt.

Candlelight flickered over his broad, smooth chest.

Shadows hugged the ridges of hard muscle. She felt she'd swoon at the sight.

Before she had a chance, he was with her, his warm skin touching hers, his arms enveloping her. His lips descended on hers, teasing, claiming. Her nipples rubbed against his chest. His fingers stroked over her stomach and back, finally finding the zipper of her skirt. He pulled it down and pushed the skirt and slip over her hips. They puddled on the floor at her feet. But instead of removing her panty hose, too, he moved his hands over her, caressing her backside, the rough skin of his hands scraping nylon. He worked his hand lower, his fingers brushing between her legs.

A shudder rippled through her. His fingers moved deeper. His touch grew more intimate, tracing her tender folds, circling the tight bundle of nerves, teasing until she couldn't take any more.

She slipped her fingers under the waistband of her panty hose and began pushing them down.

He grabbed her wrists. "Not so fast."

"I want you to touch me. I want—"

"I'll give you everything you want and more. Believe me, darlin'. I want this to last all night." He touched his lips to hers, soft, hot and full of promises.

She released the panty hose and moved her hands around his neck.

His hand once again slipped down her back and between her legs. He caressed her through the nylon, stoking her desire until she thought she'd burn up from the heat. He scattered kisses over her neck and collarbone. Then his mouth moved lower, over one breast, claiming a nipple. His tongue teased. His fingers stroked.

Her body convulsed and shuddered. She dug her fingers into his shoulders, clinging to him as her knees threatened to buckle. Heat washed through her in waves.

When the sensations finally passed, she was breathless. He kissed her cheeks, her eyelids, her lips. Then he lowered her to the bed, stripping off her panty hose on the way.

She lay back on the softness. Her muscles felt limp, her energy spent. But her heart felt strong and full to bursting.

Maybe Kelly and Cara were right. Maybe she had a bit of Shotgun Sally in her, as well. Maybe Bart was her Zachary Gale, and she was meant to save him from this murder charge. Maybe fate had brought them together and led them to this moment. She reached out her arms to him, wanting him to join her on the bed. Wanting to curl into his warmth.

"Not yet. I want to look at you." He stood at her feet, his gaze moving over her the same way his hands had done. Over her breasts, down her belly and settling between her legs. Caressing, stoking the fire once again. Finally he moved his hands to his waist and unhooked his silver buckle.

Lindsey watched, anticipation building like a coil tightening inside her.

He unzipped his fly and pushed jeans down powerful legs. Stepping out of his boots and jeans, he straightened and hooked his thumbs in the waistband of his briefs. Eyes locked with hers, he pushed them down, as well.

She lowered her gaze and swallowed into a dry throat.

She'd known from the bulge in his jeans that he was large. But she hadn't expected this. Warmth rushed between her legs. At the same time, her muscles clenched in apprehension.

The shadow of a smile played on Bart's lips. ''Don't worry. We'll take it slow. I want this to be good for you.'' He leaned forward. Starting with her feet, he massaged his way up her legs, littering kisses along the way. By the time he reached the tops of her thighs, her apprehension was gone, and tingling warmth flowed through her body.

He gently parted her legs and lowered his head. His lips caressed her. His tongue opened her.

Tension once again built in her muscles. Except this time it wasn't caused by trepidation. This time it was urgency, need. She raised her hips to him.

Cupping her buttocks in his hands, he devoured her.

Another shudder ripped through her. And another. Finally, when she was certain she couldn't take any more pleasure, he kissed his way up her body, over her breasts. He reached past her and pulled a packet from the nightstand. Ripping the condom package open, he sheathed himself before settling his hips between her spread legs.

She could feel him nestle against her, long and hard and ready. Her body ached for him to fill her. She tilted her hips, opening to him.

Claiming her lips in a kiss, he eased into her. First just a little. Then a little more.

She stretched to receive him. Pain burned through her. She sucked in a breath.

Bart froze. "I'm sorry."

She grasped his shoulders. "No. Don't stop. Please, don't stop."

He eased in a bit more.

Her body warmed, accepting him a little at a time until he was fully inside.

He searched her eyes. "Are you okay?"

Raising her chin, she pecked his lips. "I'm wonderful."

He smiled. "Yes, you are." He lowered his mouth onto hers and began moving slowly.

The pain between her legs faded, replaced by heat and wetness and overpowering need. She moved with him, awkwardly at first, then with the rhythm of a perfect dance. Heat built between them, melding their bodies, their souls. And when the shudder claimed her this time, he was with her, calling out her name.

ARM CURLED AROUND a sleeping Lindsey, Bart stared at his bedroom wall. He breathed in the light fragrance of roses, his chest aching like he'd been stuck with a dull knife.

Making love with her had been even more than he'd imagined it could be. She had touched his heart, touched his soul. She had widened his world and opened up a future he'd only dreamed of. A future filled with love and children and happily ever after.

A future he doubted he would ever know.

She'd said she wanted him, needed him, even if it only meant one night. But he couldn't fool himself. He hadn't gone against his better judgment for Lindsey's sake. He'd done it for himself. Because he needed to feel her skin against his. Because he needed to look into her eyes as he entered her. Because he needed to lock the memory of making love to her inside his heart where nothing could take it away—not the law, not prison, not the bleak future he faced. And now he'd have to live with what he'd done.

And hope to God Lindsey didn't pay the price for his selfishness.

He drew in another deep breath of her. A faint scent registered in the back of his mind. Not just the sweet fragrance of roses, but a trace of smoke. An uneasy feeling spread over his skin.

Gently untangling himself from her, he slipped from the bed and padded to the open window on bare feet. The ranch sprawled in front of him, moonlight reflecting off white buildings and pipe corrals. He inhaled again. Definitely smoke. Smoke coming from the direction of the barns.

A panicked equine scream pierced the air.

Adrenaline slammed through his bloodstream. He spun from the window. Groping in the dim light, he pulled on his clothes.

Lindsey stirred and sat up in bed. "What's going on?"

Another whinny split the night.

Bart reached for a boot. "Smells like fire. I think

it's coming from the barns. I'm going down to check it out.''

She threw back the covers and jumped out of bed, the moonlight glowing on her skin. ''I'm coming with you.''

The thought of Lindsey anywhere near a barn fire rammed into his gut like a hard fist. ''No, stay here. Call 9-1-1.''

She nodded. Struggling into her white silk blouse, she grabbed the phone at the side of the bed.

Bart finished thrusting his feet into his second boot and charged into the hall. He raced down the steps and out the door. The smoke was stronger out in the open air. He launched into a dead run. By the time he reached the door of the main horse barn, a ruckus of whinnies had started up. It was a fire, all right, in the horse barn. He had to get the horses out.

He flattened a palm against the door. The steel was cool to the touch. A good sign. At least the fire wasn't right behind the door; he had a chance to get inside. He grabbed the door's handle.

''The fire department is on its way,'' Lindsey shouted breathlessly from behind him. ''What should I do? How can I help?''

He spun around.

She was dressed in the white blouse and dark blue skirt she'd worn to court. Under the skirt, her bare legs tapered down to a pair of flimsy high-heeled shoes. Not exactly the gear for fighting fires. Not that he'd let her take one step inside that burning building even if she was dressed in full firefighter's gear. "Go wake Gary and the hands. If they aren't awake already."

She nodded and raced in the direction of the bunkhouse and apartments. The hands' living quarters were farther from the horse barns than the main house was, but Bart hoped they had heard some of the ruckus or smelled smoke and were on their way.

As soon as Lindsey had cleared out, he turned back to the barn and slid the big door open. Smoke billowed out. A wave of sound hit him. Horse snorts and screams. The thunk of hooves against wood. The low roar of flame.

He plunged into the smoke. Groping through the darkness, he located the switch box and flipped on all the lights. Even with the lights blaring overhead, the barn was dim. Smoke hung in the air and made his eyes sting and water. Smoke and something else.

The smell of gasoline.

Someone had set the fire deliberately. His gut clenched, tight as a fist. He pushed the anger from his mind. He had only minutes, maybe seconds to save the horses. He had to focus.

He raced down the barn aisle. Smoke billowed from the tack room and spread out along one wall. There were only thirty horses in this barn. Mostly his show horses, a few pregnant broodmares and a few mares with brand-new babies. The working horses and other broodmares were in the corrals outside, safe from the fire. Reaching the first box stall, he unlatched the door and yanked it open.

The mare inside nearly ran him over in her haste to

get out. He stepped back and spread his arms, barring her from running deeper into the barn, directing her toward the open door and freedom.

She weaved, undecided at first. Then finally catching a whiff of fresh air, she raced like a bat out of hell for the door, steel-shod hooves clattering and slipping on the cement aisle floor.

He moved to the next stall and the next, freeing each horse, directing them to the open door. As he got deeper into the barn, the smoke grew thicker, the heat more intense. Flames flickered and glowed, leaping over ceiling beams and huddling along the floor.

A male voice shouted through the thick smoke. *Gary.*

"I'm about halfway down!" Bart yelled back. His chest seized with the effort, sending him into a fit of coughing.

Suddenly many people were with him, pulling open stalls, herding the horses to safety. The smoke was so thick he couldn't see faces. All he could see were shapes.

One grabbed a hose in the wash stall and sprayed, flame cowering under the assault. Another sprayed a fire extinguisher. A smaller figure clad in white and dark blue slipped past, heading for the broodmare stalls at the far end of the barn.

Lindsey.

Fear clogged his throat and turned his stomach. He set out after her, racing deeper into the barn. White swirled around him, thick and lethal. He fought to see, fought to breathe. Lindsey was nowhere. It was like she'd disappeared into the white fog. Or like she'd never existed.

Had she really slipped past him into the smoke? Had he just imagined her? Imagined her because he was so scared she'd get caught up in the fire? That she'd be in danger? That he'd lose her?

Sweat poured down his face, salt and smoke filling his eyes. He fought on. If Lindsey was in here, he'd find her. Find her or die trying.

Chapter Thirteen

Bart groped through the smoke, struggling to see. The stall doors gaped open like screaming mouths on either side of the aisle. Stall after stall was empty, each horse safely outside.

No sign of Lindsey.

Even through the thickening smoke, he could see the large sliding door at this end of the barn. If he opened the door, he could have more oxygen. He could breathe. Problem was, the fire could breathe, too. He had to check the last stalls before he opened the door. Because once he opened it, he'd better damn well be prepared to get the hell out.

He forced his feet to move to the end of the barn. In spite of the hands' success in beating back the flames with the wash-rack hose, the fire was still going strong. Heat assaulted him. His lungs ached with lack of oxygen and burned from smoke. He had to get out of here. And he had to get out now.

He made his way to the end of the aisle. The end stalls were broodmare stalls, extra large and reserved for mares either with foals or expecting. He liked to

call them family double wides. They held two mares
who could drop their foals any moment. He reached
one stall and peered inside. Smoke burned his eyes.
Tears streamed down his cheeks. But through the
tears, he could see the stall was empty.

He started across the aisle to the other side of the
barn. Before he reached the last stall, he could sense
movement inside. He raced through the open door.

Lindsey stood near the head of the sorrel mare.

Bart's heart caught in his throat.

Her eyes were wide, her hair singed. She grasped
the mare's mane with one hand, obviously trying to
coax the frightened horse out of the false safety of the
stall. When she saw Bart, a look of relief washed over
her face. "She's scared. She made it halfway down
the aisle and then turned around and headed back to
her stall. I think she might be in labor. I can't leave
her here."

Of course she couldn't. Not Lindsey. Hell, neither
could he.

The mare's wet sides heaved. Her eyes rolled white
in their sockets.

He slipped into the stall and joined Lindsey at the
mare's head. "We need something to cover her eyes.
If she can't see the fire, she won't know what she's
going through." He stripped off his shirt and tied it
over the mare's eyes.

The mare tossed her head, trying to rid herself of
the blindfold. He grasped a handful of mane. Using it
as a lead rope, he guided the mare to the mouth of the
stall while Lindsey encouraged her from behind.

The mare balked at the door. Lindsey raised a flat hand and brought it down on her haunches in a loud slap. The mare surged out the door and into the aisle.

Bart gripped her mane tighter and circled an arm under her neck to bring her back under control. He guided the blinded horse to the barn door. He glanced at Lindsey. "Open it. And as soon as you do, get out. I'll be right behind. This side of the barn is going to be a fireball."

She nodded. She grabbed the handle of the door. At Bart's nod, she yanked it wide and jumped out. The mare shot through the opening, pulling Bart with her. Flame roared behind them, heat licking at their heels.

BART SURVEYED the ranch, anger hardening in his chest. Red and blue light throbbed in the night, bouncing off the whitewashed buildings and fence like the sign announcing some damn sale at the local discount store. The county's fire truck, all five county sheriff's cars and an ambulance crowded around the charred skeleton that was once the horse barn.

The hands who weren't being treated by the EMS for burns and smoke inhalation had gathered the horses into one of the far corrals. Their frightened whinnies cut through the low rumble of human voices.

He turned from the wreckage and focused on Lindsey. Perched inside the open back door of the ambulance, she stared at the activity with shell-shocked eyes. Despite the warm night, a blanket was wrapped around her shoulders. She held it tight at her throat with trembling hands.

It'd been damn foolish, the way she'd plunged into the smoke to save that mare without thought of the risk to herself. And damn brave. But he'd come to expect nothing less from her. He just hoped to hell her bravery didn't get her hurt. Or dead.

A sheriff's car pulled up to the ambulance on its way out. Bart recognized the black hair and sharp cheekbones of Deputy Mitchell Steele behind the wheel. He motioned for Mitch to stop.

Mitch hung an arm out his open window. "Bart."

"Mitch, I need a word."

The deputy looked up at him, narrowing his unusual golden eyes. "What is it?"

"I smelled gasoline. In the barn. When I opened the door it hit me like a damned blanket."

"So you think it's arson?"

He nodded. "Listen, could you do me a favor? Could you check on Kenny's whereabouts tonight? A lot of things have been happening around here since Jeb's death, things I suspect Kenny is behind, and Hurley won't look into any of it."

Mitch nodded as if he wasn't surprised. "I'll check up on Kenny and see what else I can do. But I can't promise much. Sheriff Ben and Hurley have been keeping out of the loop lately. Probably has something to do with the upcoming election. Ben has his eye on the mayor's job, and Hurley doesn't want me as competition for the sheriff post."

"He's worried you're going to follow in your daddy's footsteps?"

A shadow of pain passed over Mitch's hard face.

Pain, no doubt, from the rumors surrounding Mitch's father's death. Rumors of scandal and suicide.

"I'd appreciate it if you'd do whatever you can, Mitch. You're the only lawman in this county that I trust."

"And we all know how much the trust of a murderer is worth, don't we?" Hurley Zeller strode toward them on short legs. He turned his mean little eyes on Mitch. "This is my case, Steele. Don't you have a call to get to?"

The planes of Mitch's face hardened. He glanced at the beat-up sedan pulling up the road to the ranch. Cara Hamilton's red hair shone in the passenger seat, her boss Beau Jennings hulked behind the wheel. "Don't worry, Hurley. I'm not planning to steal your headlines. We'll talk later, Bart." Mitch raised the car's window and drove away.

Hurley cursed at the departing car and then swung his attention back to Bart. "So what were you talking to Steele about? Confessing you set the fire yourself to direct attention away from your uncle's murder? You know, make yourself look more sympathetic and heroic to the public?"

"I hope you either have facts to back up those charges or you keep them to yourself, Deputy," Lindsey said as she stepped beside Bart. Her voice challenged despite the pallor of her face and trembling of her hands. "That is unless you want to be looking at a lawsuit once Bart is acquitted."

"I'm just calling it as I see it. I'm sure you two

have some scheme cooked up, but I sure as hell ain't playing along.'' Hurley's lip curled in a sneer.

A sneer Bart would love to wipe off with his fists.

Lindsey shook her head like she couldn't believe what she was hearing. "What is it with you? What do you have against Bart?"

"Other than the fact that he murdered a man?"

"He didn't kill Jeb Rawlins."

"Right. What you and this whole damn town don't seem to understand is that just because Bart was a football star in high school, and he's been Mustang Valley's goddamn golden boy all the years since, doesn't mean he's better than the rest of us. Doesn't mean he gets away with murder, either. And I'm going to make damn sure of it."

Bart's blood heated to boiling. "So that's what it comes down to, Hurley? You've been waiting all these years to pay me back for beating you out for quarterback in high school?"

"I didn't put the knife in your hand and aim you at Jeb's throat. I'll enjoy bringing you down, but you're the one who made it happen. And if the fire inspector finds you had anything to do with this, I'll be right there to arrest you for insurance fraud and arson." The deputy walked away, each stride exaggerated like a puffed-up rooster.

Bart raked a hand through his hair. "Hell, I wouldn't put it past Hurley to frame me for the fire."

She raised her chin. Determination glinted in her eyes. "I'm going to have a talk with Cara. Maybe Hurley isn't concerned about the life and property of a defendant in a murder trial, but I'll bet Sheriff Ben will care about what the press has to say. Especially with an election coming up in the fall.''

Bart watched her stride off. The blanket flared out behind her like some damn superhero cape. If anyone could twist Ben and Hurley's arms, it would be Lindsey and Cara. They were just lucky Kelly Lansing had left on her honeymoon, and they only had two of the dynamic trio to contend with.

Bart looked down the driveway in the direction of Mitch Steele's fading taillights. He hoped Mitch could dig something up to nail Kenny. Of course, even if he did, Sheriff Ben was still in charge. And press or no press, the sheriff would favor Hurley's word over Mitch's any day. Hadn't his failed attempts to reach Mitch before this already proved that? Hadn't Mitch himself said the sheriff and Hurley had purposely kept him away from Bart's case?

A chill worked over his chest and back. The truth was, no matter what Cara wrote in the paper, no matter which deputy was on the case, Bart couldn't expect protection from Sheriff Ben. Not for his dad or Lindsey or the cowboys, horses and cattle who lived on the Four Aces.

He thought of Lindsey. Of the way she'd given herself to him last night. Of the way she'd risked her neck to save the broodmare. Of the way she'd stood toe-to-toe with Hurley to defend him with all the fire of an avenging angel. If anything happened to her...if anything happened to Daddy or Gary or the other hands and their families...he would never forgive himself. If there was anything he'd learned through this ordeal it was that people were precious. More precious than unfulfilled dreams or family legacies. More precious than wide-open spaces and white pipe fence. A lot of people on this ranch relied on him, and it was up to Bart to make sure they were safe.

Or at least to take away the reason they were in danger.

"ARE YOU ALL RIGHT, Bart?" Paul Lambert's brow pinched in a concerned frown. He swung the door to his office wide and ushered Bart inside like he was royalty.

Or some kind of invalid.

"I'm fine."

"I heard about the fire at the Four Aces. It was a miracle you didn't lose any horses. Or people."

Bart nodded. It was barely ten o'clock in the morning, but by now he had no doubt every soul in Mustang Valley had heard about last night's fire. "Guess I've been providing the town's entertainment lately."

The pity on Paul's face stung.

Bart shifted his boots on the thick carpet. Hell, he didn't need pity. He, Lindsey, Gary and all the hands had gotten by unhurt. They'd managed to save all the horses. What they hadn't saved was the barn itself. Or Bart's confidence that he could protect his dad or Lindsey or anyone else, for that matter. Especially if he was operating from a jail cell.

A shiver worked its way over his skin. If he hadn't seen Lindsey through the smoke…

He shut the image from his mind. He couldn't think about how close he'd come to losing her. He could only focus on what had brought him to Lambert & Church. "I didn't come about the fire, Paul. I need to talk to you."

"What about?"

Bart took his hat from his singed hair and tried to beat back his misgivings. He hated not telling Lindsey what he was doing, but he couldn't take the chance that she would talk him out of it. "The other day you said you had someone interested in buying the Four Aces."

"You want to sell?"

Bart bobbed his head. Pain threaded through his chest with every beat of his heart.

"Why don't you sit down?"

Hat in hand, Bart forced himself to walk to the desk. The soles of his boots bogged down in the plush carpet. The office's air-freshener scent clogged his throat, still sore from smoke. When he reached the chairs in front of Paul's desk, he balked. Somehow the thought of sinking into one of those chairs seemed like he was giving up.

Paul circled his desk, his shrewd eyes sizing up the situation. "You seem hesitant."

Hesitant about selling his dreams? His legacy for future generations of Rawlins children? Rawlins children that would never be born? He shook his head. "I don't have much of a choice."

Paul arched his brows. "This isn't about your case, is it? Lindsey might be a little green, but she's a competent attorney. The law is in her blood. You'll see when you get to trial.''

"I don't doubt Lindsey. Not for one second.''

"Then what's the problem?''

He didn't want to tell Paul more. Not today. Not when he felt that every word of explanation tore away a little bit of his soul. "Do you want to talk business? Or should I call Brandy Carmichael and list the ranch with her?''

At mention of Brandy's name, Paul froze. Guilt showed clear as day on his face along with a touch of anger. Apparently the cheerleader-turned-Realtor was telling the truth about their personal history. "I can call my client right now, if you like, set up a meeting.''

The air seemed to rush from the room. Bart struggled to take a breath. He had to do this. If he wanted to keep Lindsey safe, keep his dad safe, keep the hands and their families safe, he needed to say goodbye to the only home he'd ever known.

A small price to pay. "Do it.''

LINDSEY SORTED through the papers and unopened mail cluttering her desk. She couldn't stand working in this kind of mess. She liked the desktop clear, organized, professional. Especially since her life had been anything but clear, organized and professional since she'd walked into the Mustang Valley jail and shaken hands with Bart.

Her throat ached at the thought of him. His strength and cool head when he'd helped her rescue the broodmare from the fire. The pain she'd seen in his eyes as he watched the smoldering skeleton of his prized horse barn. The way he so obviously cared about every cowboy and horse and cow who lived on the ranch as if they were part of his family.

The way he cared about *her*.

A tingle traveled over her body. Last night he'd said he wanted to show her how deeply and thoroughly a man could love a woman. He had done just that and more. And now the future seemed more muddled than ever.

She picked up the stack of mail that had just arrived this morning and forced her mind off Bart and onto work. She flipped through the letters. A request for a court date here, a note from her mother there. A plain white envelope caught her attention. A Fort Worth postmark canceled the stamp. Her pulse picked up its pace.

Fitting a nail under the flap, she ripped it open. Tissue-thin paper spilled out. The drug report. Holding her breath, she unfolded it and skimmed the page. One word leaped out at her. The word listed in the results column of each test.

Negative.

She closed her eyes and covered her face with her hands.

"My God, Lindsey. Are you okay?"

Lindsey wiped silent tears from the corners of her eyes and focused on Nancy standing in the doorway. "I'm fine."

"I heard about the fire at the Four Aces. How terrible. Shouldn't you be home recovering?"

Although Nancy seemed like a nice woman, she had never acted personally concerned about Lindsey since she had taken the job at Lambert & Church. Wouldn't you know her maternal instincts would pick now to kick in? Now, when Lindsey desperately needed to be alone. "I'm fine, Nancy. Really."

The older woman tapped herself on the forehead as if remembering something. "The meeting, of course. I suppose you had to come in for the meeting this morning."

"Meeting?"

"With Roger Rosales from the Ranger Corporation."

She gave Nancy a blank look.

"Don't you know?"

Lindsey shook her head.

"I realize you're acting as Bart Rawlins's criminal attorney. But I just assumed you were involved with this, too. Or you'd know about it, at the very least." She shook her head, flustered, and pressed her lips tightly closed as if determined not to let another word escape.

"What was the meeting about, Nancy?"

The office administrator's eyes shifted to the door. She looked like she wanted to bolt.

"What was the meeting about?" she repeated. "I'm Bart's attorney. You can tell me."

"I don't know."

"Suit yourself. But if you don't dish, I'm going to

have to walk down the hall and ask Paul. He'll want to know where I got wind of the meeting and..."

"All right, all right. It's about Bart's ranch, the Four Aces. He's selling."

"And Ranger Corporation is buying," Lindsey said flatly. She wrapped her arms around herself and willed her body not to start shaking.

Chapter Fourteen

"You can't sell the ranch."

Bart stopped in his tracks in front of the corral and turned to face Lindsey. He knew she'd find out. She was too smart, too resourceful for him to be able to keep her in the dark long. "I have to sell, Lindsey. It's the only way."

"The only way to do what?"

"Protect you, Daddy, Gary, the hands and their families, everyone. You read that message spray-painted on your car. My God, you were attacked in your apartment. Anyone who's around me is in danger. If I sell, it'll break the connection."

"It won't break the connection between you and your father. Or you and me."

"No." He looked past her and focused on the spot where Gary's bay mare stood tied to the corral fence, saddled and ready. "I'm still figuring a way to deal with that."

"You don't have to sell the ranch. Hire security."

"For the next twenty-five years to life?"

"You're not going to be convicted."

He shook his head and brought his gaze back to her. Determination burned in her eyes, hot as blue flame. Her hands balled into fists by her side like she was ready to challenge the entire Mustang Valley legal system to a brawl in order to save his hide. ''You've seen for yourself how the law works in this county. Hurley might or might not be crooked, but he definitely has a grudge against me. And he has definitely stacked the deck.''

Concern flashed in her eyes. She glanced away, a split second too late.

''What? What's happened?''

''I got the drug analysis from the lab. Blood and urine.''

He didn't have to hear her answer to know what the report said. He steeled himself for the blow. ''There was no Rohypnol, was there? Or anything else.''

''No.''

He met the news without flinching. ''Selling the place is the right thing to do. The only thing I can do.''

She shook her head and raised her chin. ''No. I'll find another way to prove you're innocent. I can win an acquittal. You have to believe in me.''

''I do believe in *you*. But I can't ignore the evidence stacked against me.''

She shook her head. ''My family always says they believe in me, too. But they don't act like it. You don't, either.''

''It isn't a matter of believing in you, Lindsey. I just can't take the chance someone will be hurt. That you'll be hurt. People are more important than a ranch. Even this ranch.''

She looked away from him, glancing past the horse tied to the fence and toward the apartments beyond. Two little kids galloped around like colts in front of the long, low building. When she looked back to him, the fire in her eyes was barely a smolder. ''You're right. This has nothing to do with me. And you have no other choice.''

A knife of pain stabbed into his chest at the defeat in her voice, in her eyes. He reached out and pulled her into his arms. ''The way your family tries to protect you and help you has nothing to do with not believing in you, either, Lindsey. They worry about you because they love you.''

She looked up at him and searched his eyes. ''And you? Why do you worry about me, Bart?''

His throat closed. He touched her hair, her face, and then let his hand fall to his side. Swallowing hard, he pulled back and turned away. He couldn't look into her eyes one more second. Couldn't stand to see the love shining there. The kind of love he'd seen in his mama's eyes every time she looked at his daddy. The kind of forever love he'd have given his soul for before he'd been charged with Jeb's murder.

He focused on Gary's mare. A halter and lead rope secured her to the fence. A brand new bridle draped over the saddle horn. The bit and reins rested against the pro rodeo logo tooled into the saddle's fender.

A dose of adrenaline slammed into his bloodstream. ''That saddle.''

Lindsey glanced at the saddle and then back to him, her eyebrows dipping low in question.

"The saddle on Gary's mare. It's the one he won back when he was riding the rodeo circuit."

"I'm not following."

"It's his favorite saddle. He kept it in the tack room of the horse barn."

Understanding dawned. Her eyes widened. "The saddle should have burned along with everything else in the tack room."

He nodded. "Unless Gary took it out..." He didn't want to believe where his mind was taking him.

"...before he started the fire..." Lindsey finished for him.

LINDSEY STOOD behind Bart as he slipped his key into Gary's apartment door. Despite the fact that his horse was tied to the corral fence, the foreman was nowhere to be found. And he didn't answer the knock on his door.

She thought of the pain on Bart's face when he recognized what the saddle meant. Duplicity. Betrayal. If only they could call the sheriff, let the law deal with Gary. It would be easier on Bart than confronting his foreman personally. But Hurley hadn't taken the fire seriously in the first place. Calling him would yield nothing but the joy of dealing with his bad attitude. No, they had to get evidence of Gary's involvement. Once they did that, Hurley and the sheriff would have no choice but to pursue the case.

The knob turned under Bart's hand and he swung

the door wide. The room was dim, blinds drawn against the morning sun. "Gary? You home?"

The apartment was silent as death.

Bart flicked on a light and stepped into the living room.

Lindsey followed, glancing around the room, looking for some clue to the man who lived there. But except for a worn couch and small television, the room was nearly empty. No sign of Gary. Not much sign of life in general. At least not much of a life. "How well do you know Gary?"

"He started working here when I was just a kid. He taught me practically everything I know about ranching. He's been like a brother."

Like a brother. His words tore at Lindsey's heart. The strain on Bart was worse than she'd imagined. Much worse. "Maybe he didn't do anything. Maybe there's another explanation for the saddle."

"If there is, I sure as hell can't come up with it. And I've been trying. God, have I been trying."

Her heart ached for him. "But why would he burn the horse barn?"

Bart flinched with obvious pain. "I wish I *couldn't* think of a reason."

She watched him with questioning eyes and willed him to go on.

"When my daddy passed the ranch to me, he gave a portion to Gary for his retirement. Sweat equity."

"So he'll profit when you sell."

Bart nodded. "He's been wanting to retire for a

long time now. Bad back. He may have thought a fire would hurry up the sale. If he did, he was right.''

''But if he wanted the money to retire, why wouldn't he just ask you to buy him out?''

''He did. Only problem was cash flow. I couldn't scare up the money to give him what his share is worth. And with beef prices the way they've been for the past ten years, the bank refused to loan me that much. The Four Aces is a successful operation, but that's only because we've cut the fat to the bone. It'll take me years to get the kind of money Gary deserved. He knew that.''

''Why wouldn't he just sell to someone else?''

''My daddy stipulated that he could only sell back to a Rawlins. He wanted to keep the ranch in the family. Maybe he shouldn't have done that. Maybe he should have given Gary more of a way out.'' He drew in a pained breath. ''I guess the only way we're going to get answers is to start looking.''

She nodded. They needed answers, all right. She just hoped the answers they found wouldn't bring Bart more anguish.

They moved quickly through the apartment. The place was painstakingly neat, making a search easy— a search that turned up a couple of sticks of furniture, a few dishes and some work clothes. In other words, nothing.

''There's one other place he stores things. Follow me.''

They retraced their steps. Once outside, Bart headed for a garage to the rear of the apartment building. He pulled up the door. Sunlight flooded the space, illuminating everything from an old sofa and chair to stacks of boxes to spare tires.

Bart picked his way through the garage to a row of cabinets lining the back wall. "This one's Gary's." He opened one of the doors. Color drained from his face. "Damn."

"What is it?" Lindsey moved up behind him. A can of spray paint peeked out over some old truck parts on the top shelf. The cap was bright red. She sucked in a breath. Here, the entire time they'd been looking for Gary that night, he'd been vandalizing her car.

But Bart wasn't looking at the spray paint. His attention was riveted on a lower shelf.

She craned her neck to see around him. Tucked behind some odds and ends was a small black box. "What is it?"

"The ELT for the helicopter." He clipped off the words. A muscle twitched along his jaw.

"Gary sabotaged the helicopter?"

Bart closed his eyes as if struggling to hold on to his self-control. "How could he have done it? How could he have tried to kill us?"

"And your father? Do you think he let your father out on the range?"

Judging from the anger radiating from him, he did. He grimaced and pressed a thumb and forefinger to his closed eyelids, as if by doing so, he could erase what he'd seen—he could erase Gary's betrayal. "After all Daddy did for him. How could he have done it? And for what? Money? When I get my hands on that bastard—'' He opened his eyes and froze, staring at a spot among the clutter on the floor.

A trickle of fear ran down Lindsey's spine. "What is it?"

Bart closed his eyes again. "It's Gary."

She stepped around Bart. "Where is—" Her question caught in her throat.

Gary lay on his side among a jumble of boxes, an arm stretched out toward them. A pool of red puddled under his body.

Lindsey's stomach heaved. "Oh, God."

Before she could turn away, a car swung around the burned wreckage of the horse barn, gravel popping under its tires. Blue and red lights flashed from its roof. Another sheriff's car followed.

"Oh, hell," Bart muttered.

Hurley scrambled out of the first car. A deputy Lindsey didn't recognize climbed from the second and fell in behind him. Struggling to regain her composure, Lindsey took a step toward them. "We were just about to call you, Deputy."

Hurley looked past her. "What the hell do we have here?" Eyes narrowing, he rested his hand on the butt of his gun. Behind him, the other deputy did the same.

Chapter Fifteen

Bart leaned back in the hard chair and tried to smother the worry building inside him like a raging brushfire. The tiny office in the Mustang Valley police station closed in on him. The dark lens of the camera in the corner of the room stared down on him. It hadn't taken much to figure that Hurley would try to pin Gary's death on him. He'd seen that coming the moment the weaselly deputy had roared up the ranch road, lights flashing. What he couldn't figure out was how Hurley knew about Gary. And where he'd taken Lindsey.

Finally, after letting Bart stew for at least an hour, Hurley pushed open the door and stepped inside. Cradling a thick folder in the crook of his arm, he crossed the tiny room in two steps. He dropped the folder on the desk with a thump and stood over Bart, hands on hips. "Who'd a thunk it'd end like this, eh, Bart?"

Bart tried his best to stifle a growl. "Where's Lindsey? I want to see my lawyer."

"We'll get to that. First you got to tell me why you killed Gary. Did he find out about your plan to kill

Jeb and take his ranch? Or was Gary in on it with you?''

"Gary was the one who vandalized Lindsey's car. He sabotaged the helicopter. He burned down the horse barn. He may have killed Jeb, too, for all I know. Look in his garage space. The evidence is all there.''

"And that's why you killed him? You thought he did all these things?''

"I didn't kill Gary.''

"Don't play me for a fool, Rawlins. I know damned well you killed Gary. I drove up while you were busy stashing the body, remember? Or did you kill him earlier, and you were just planting the evidence you mentioned when I drove up?''

Bart's head throbbed. "When you drove up, I'd just discovered the body.''

"Right.''

"Ask Lindsey.''

Hurley rolled his beady eyes. "I'll just rush off and do that.''

"Where is she?''

"That shouldn't be your concern right now, Bart. You should be focused on explaining your ass out of this mess.''

Bart narrowed his eyes. "How did you happen to be out at the ranch at just that moment anyway, Hurley?''

"I came to question you.''

"If you didn't know Gary was already dead and you weren't setting me up to take the blame, what were you planning to question me about?''

"You really are a good actor, Bart. You should have gone out for theater in high school instead of football."

"I'm telling the truth, damn it."

"Right." The deputy stroked his chin. "But then, I suppose you don't know we found her."

"Found who?"

Hurley stared at him, a smug grin on his face.

Bart wanted to wipe that grin off more than he wanted air. "Tell me, damn it."

"Like you don't already know. Unless there are more bodies out there we ain't found yet."

A body. Someone else was dead. *"Tell me."*

"Pretty smart to send us on a wild-goose chase looking for Beatrice Jensen when she's been in the Squaw Creek Reservoir all along."

Beatrice. He tried to catch his breath. Jeb, Beatrice, Gary...all dead. And Hurley wanted to believe *he* had murdered them. His mind spun. He gripped the chair arms.

"You'd be better off confessing, Bart." Hurley said, his voice suddenly soft with kindness. "The whole thing will go easier on you if you tell us what happened. Make us understand."

"I didn't kill Beatrice, Hurley. You've got to believe me."

Hurley let out a frustrated breath. "You have no idea what you're up against."

Bart's gut clenched. "What? What am I up against? Who's doing this? Who's paying you to railroad me?",

The little deputy looked down at him and shook his

head, the disgust at Bart's suggestion plain on his face. "The justice system, Bart. You're up against the Texas justice system. Murderers don't go free around here like they do in bleeding-heart states like California. Here they get the needle. And that's what you're going to get if you don't do something to help yourself."

Bart knew all about the Texas death penalty. He'd even been in favor of it once. Before he knew how easily a man could be railroaded for a crime he didn't commit. Before he knew how easily *he* could be railroaded. "Where's Lindsey? I want to talk to my lawyer."

"No lawyer is going to get you off. You've killed more than one person now. And the way I see it, those murders are all linked to your scheme to get your hands on Jeb's land. I just talked to the D.A. before coming in here. And he promised me he was going for the death penalty."

Bart gritted his teeth. He remembered Lindsey's explanation of the capital murder laws the day he'd met her in the Mustang County jail. And far as he could tell, Hurley was telling the truth. "I want to talk to my lawyer, and I want to talk to her *now*."

"You can talk to your lawyer all you want, but it ain't going to be Lindsey Wellington no more."

Fear stabbed into Bart's gut. "Why not? What happened to her?"

Hurley leaned back against the wall, the smile on his face bigger than the state of Texas. "Lindsey Wellington is in the next office chatting with the sheriff.

Too bad you got her involved in this. Seems she's facing charges now too.''

''I GOT HERE as fast as I could.'' Paul Lambert stepped into the sheriff's station office and took the chair next to Bart. He gave Bart a tight smile, clearly meant to be reassuring.

Bart didn't bother smiling back. ''Is Lindsey okay?''

''Don's talking to her in the next room. He'll be taking her case. I'll take over yours, if that's okay with you.''

''Doesn't Don just do wills? Does he know how criminal law works?'' He'd never had cause to distrust Don Church and his abilities, but with the stakes so high, he had to be sure.

''Lindsey will be fine, Bart. From what I've gleaned, the sheriff's evidence of her role in the actual murder isn't too convincing.''

Maybe not, but Bart wasn't willing to take that chance. ''If the evidence isn't convincing, why is she being arrested?''

''She hasn't been arrested. And neither have you. Not yet, anyway. You're both merely here for questioning.''

''Why is she being questioned?''

''Because the sheriff has some physical evidence that suggests she helped you dispose of Beatrice Jensen's body.''

Bart sat forward in his chair and gripped the chair arms. ''That's ridiculous. What kind of evidence?''

"That I don't know."

"Well, you'd better damn well find out, Paul."

Paul stuck his hands out, palms to Bart, fingers splayed. "Don is handling Lindsey's case. He'll take care of her. You need to calm down."

Bart couldn't calm down. Not with Lindsey in trouble. It was one thing for the law in this county to railroad him, but he wasn't going to sit by and pretend to be civilized while they railroaded Lindsey. "What is she facing?"

"Possible accessory-to-murder charges."

Bart jolted from the chair. This couldn't be happening. He stepped forward to pace, but there wasn't enough space in the cramped room to take more than a couple steps.

"Don't panic, Bart. I can't see this going too far. The idea of Lindsey being involved is ludicrous. They're just rattling their sabers."

He spun back to face Paul. "You don't think they'll indict her?"

The lawyer grimaced. "They might. But that doesn't mean they have a case. The grand jury is the prosecution's own private dog-and-pony show. Marshall could probably convince the grand jurors to indict a ham sandwich, as the courthouse saying goes."

"She could face a trial? Prison?"

Paul held up a hand. "I doubt the charges will stick. Not from what I've heard of their evidence."

"What about her career?"

"It depends on a lot of factors. If she's indicted, she could face disbarment."

Paul's words hit him like a mule kick to the head. He tried to breathe. Lindsey's career was her life. Being disbarred would kill her. He couldn't let that happen. "What if I confess? What if I say I did it all without Lindsey knowing about any of it?"

Paul shook his head. "You're facing the death penalty now, Bart—multiple murders committed pursuant to the same scheme or course of conduct. You confess, and you're putting yourself on death row."

"Isn't there a good chance of that happening no matter what I do?"

Paul grimaced again and looked to the floor, obviously not wanting to answer.

"Isn't there, Paul?"

He let out a deep sigh. "I suppose there is."

"Then I have nothing to lose." Bart drew himself up. God forgive him for the lie, but he had to do what he had to do. "Call in the D.A., Paul. I want to confess."

FINALLY ALONE, Lindsey hunched in the police station's hard wooden chair and let Don Church's visit wash through her memory. The partner had been nervous, his voice pitched a bit higher than it usually was. Especially when he got to the part about Beatrice Jensen's murder and evidence that Lindsey had helped Bart cover it up.

The way Don had looked at her, she could tell he had his doubts about her innocence. No wonder he was never a poker player. Or a litigator. Don didn't have the nerves for high-stakes games.

She pushed her hair back from her face. What Don thought didn't matter. The truth didn't seem to matter. All that mattered was seeing Bart.

What she was facing was nothing compared to what he must be going through. A triple-murder charge would qualify Bart for the death penalty. And the State of Texas took that designation seriously.

She lowered her face into her hands and stared at the floor between her fingers. A sob worked its way up her throat, emotion choking her, threatening to drag her under.

Footfalls outside the door cut through her despair. The door to the little office swung wide. But instead of Hurley Zeller's smug sneer or Don's dapper smile, a dark and handsome deputy she recognized from the aftermath of the barn fire peered down at her with the most unusual gold eyes she'd ever seen. "Lindsey Wellington?"

"Yes?"

"You're free to go."

His simple phrase sent a shock wave through her. "I'm what?"

"You're free to go."

"I'm not going to be arrested?"

"No."

Relief sagged through her. But the relief was short-lived. It didn't make sense they would let her leave just like that. Not after what Don had told her. He said they'd found her date book in the reservoir near Beatrice's body. He said they'd found mud consistent with the reservoir on a pair of shoes in her apartment.

The police didn't let that sort of thing go. It just didn't happen. "Why am I not being arrested?"

Surprise registered on the deputy's strong face. "You want to be arrested?"

"Of course not. I just want to know why I'm not, Deputy…"

"Steele. Mitchell Steele."

"Deputy Steele."

"I can't tell you why, ma'am. I don't know. The district attorney just told me you aren't."

Lindsey's mind raced. Maybe they believed Don when he told them the date book was in her stolen briefcase. Maybe the mud hadn't ended up matching that at the reservoir. But somehow she got the feeling it wasn't that simple. "What about Bart Rawlins? Is he being charged?"

The deputy pressed full lips together.

She lunged to her feet. "If I'm not being charged as his conspirator, then I'm still his lawyer. I need to know."

A muscle worked, flexing from jaw to sharp cheekbone. Finally he gave a single nod. "Bart met with the district attorney about fifteen minutes ago."

Bart met with Marshall Kramer? All Don had said was that Bart was talking to Paul. He hadn't mentioned anything about a meeting with the D.A. "And?"

"Bart cut a deal."

Her head spun. Her stomach swirled. It didn't make sense. Bart hadn't killed anyone. Why on earth would he plead guilty? "A deal? What kind of deal?"

"I don't know," Deputy Steele said. "You'll have to ask Bart. I'll take you to him."

Foreboding gripped her throat like a strong hand. She nodded.

Turning on a heel, Deputy Steele led her out of the room. He stopped at the next door in the hall, rapped on it twice and pushed it open. He stepped to the side so Lindsey could enter.

From the hard chairs to the small desk to the camera peering down from the corner, the room was identical to the one she'd just left. Bart sat beside Paul. He looked tired, drawn, his skin pale under his tan. And instead of the straightforward way he'd always met her gaze, he dodged and looked away.

A tremor shuddered through her. "Bart, I need to talk to you."

Paul pushed himself up from his chair and stepped toward her. "This isn't a good idea."

"How can it not be a good idea to talk to my client?"

"It's all right, Paul. It's only right that I tell her myself."

Paul glanced back at Bart briefly before returning his scrutiny to Lindsey. Finally giving a nod, he stepped past her and out of the room. The door thunked closed.

Lindsey dragged in a breath. "What is going on, Bart? What kind of deal did you cut with the D.A.?" Her voice came out in a choked whisper.

His lips flattened. He focused on a spot in the corner of the room, as if he couldn't bare to look at her. "I'm going to have to let you go, Lindsey. Paul is representing me now.''

Her heart stuttered. She didn't know what she'd expected him to say, but this certainly wasn't it. ''You're firing me?''

''Yes.''

The room whirled around her. ''Why?''

''Things have changed. I need a lawyer with more experience.''

She staggered back. She'd always known this was a possibility. Hadn't she suggested it to Bart herself? The fact was, criminal law wasn't her specialty. She'd never taken a case solo, let alone a murder case. She was in over her head from the beginning. The smart thing, the prudent thing for him to do would be to find a lawyer with more experience. And although Paul's current specialty was real estate law, he'd worked criminal cases before. Bart needed a lawyer like Paul.

Then why did his decision feel like the thrust of a blade into her heart?

She studied Bart. His shuttered expression. The way he looked everywhere but at her. There was more to this than he was telling. Much more. ''I can understand your decision. But if that's truly how you feel, why can't you look me in the eye?''

As if to prove her wrong, he focused on her. His eyes ached with sadness, hopelessness. And underneath she sensed something more. Something tender. Protective.

She knew Bart. And she knew what he was doing. ''You're protecting me.''

He shook his head and looked away.

"The sheriff has evidence that I was involved in disposing of Beatrice Jensen's body, and yet they didn't arrest me. They let me go." Her mind swam. Dread inched up her spine. "Bart, what did you do? What kind of deal did you agree to?"

"I'm already going to prison for killing Jeb."

"What did you do?"

"I confessed."

Lindsey tried to breathe, but she couldn't draw air through her pinched throat. "You can't confess."

"I'm not going to let them go after you just to save myself from a couple more murder charges."

"A couple more murder charges?" Panic swamped her. "Being convicted for killing three people in Texas is worlds different from being convicted for killing one. Life-and-death different."

His face was fixed as stone.

Realization closed over her head like cold, black water. "Oh, my God. That's what you want, isn't it? You want to be executed."

He dipped his head. "I'm confessing to the murders. That's all."

"That's not all, and you know it. Marshall is going to argue that those murders were committed pursuant to the same scheme or course of conduct. He's going for the death penalty. And you're giving him a confession. That's the same as committing suicide."

"It's not suicide, damn it."

"Just because it's state-sponsored and disguised as justice doesn't mean it's not suicide." She studied

Bart's face. "But you wouldn't see it that way, would you? You'd see it as sacrifice."

Bart looked up. His eyes narrowed to green slits. His expression warned her to back off.

"No. Not sacrifice. It isn't sacrifice when you do it for someone you love, is it?" She threw his words back at him with all the force she could muster. Rage stormed through her. Her heart ached. Bart loved her. She knew that now. Knew it with more certainty than she'd known anything in her life. And because he loved her, she was going to lose him.

"Life in prison is the same as death."

It all fell into place. It all made some kind of twisted sense. His need to protect her. His seeing life in prison as a death sentence. A sentence he didn't want to visit on her. "You don't want me waiting."

The planes of his face hardened.

"That's it, isn't it? You don't want me waiting like your mother waited for your father."

"Leave it alone." Every muscle in his body tensed for fight. He wasn't giving in.

God help her, the stubborn, self-sacrificing fool wasn't giving in. "For God's sake, Bart, all they have against me is a date book that was stolen with my briefcase and a little mud on a pair of my shoes—mud that hasn't even been tied to the reservoir. The best they can hope for in a case like that is a hung jury."

"But that might be enough."

"Enough for what?"

"Enough to disbar you. Enough to ruin your career."

Her career. Numbness stole through her. Numbness and despair. Once she'd thought her career was the most important thing in the world. Only now could she see how wrong she'd been. Her career was nothing without her family's love. It was nothing without Kelly and Cara's unconditional support. But most of all, it was nothing without Bart. "If saving my career means losing you, it's not worth it."

"You're a good lawyer, Lindsey. A great lawyer. You've worked so hard, wanted it so—"

"No. My mother is the one who had it right. My mother knew a career could wait, that some things are more important, some things have to come first. That all the success in the world doesn't mean a thing if you don't have someone to share it with. I want the success, Bart. But it doesn't mean anything if I can't share it with you."

"They're going to convict me anyway. I'm just trying to keep them from ruining you in the process."

Tears clogged her throat. "I'm not going to let you do this."

"You have nothing to say about it, Lindsey. You're not my lawyer anymore."

"Maybe not. But I'm not going to sit by while you let them put a needle in your arm. I'm going to the D.A. I'm going to tell him the whole thing is a lie."

"And what would that do? He won't believe you. He thinks you were helping me cover up, for God's sake."

He was right. Marshall wouldn't believe her. Not

unless she had evidence to back her up. Strong evidence. Evidence that didn't seem to exist.

Panic threatened to choke her. "I'll challenge the allocution. Judge Valenzuela won't proceed with sentencing if your former lawyer challenges the validity of your confession."

His hands opened and closed by his sides. "You can't do that."

"Actually, I can."

"And what good will it do? You'll be charged for helping me, and the D.A. will use my confession against me during the trial. The jury will convict me without a second thought." He was right. Oh, God. Her knees wobbled. And folded. She reached out, supporting herself on the back of a chair.

Suddenly Bart was beside her. His gentle hands, his fresh scent, his tenderness. He propped her up and guided her into the chair. "I'm not going to let you sacrifice your career for no reason. Please, Lindsey. Let it go."

She looked into his eyes, soaked in his touch. He was so tender, so caring, so giving. Her heart squeezed. "It really isn't a sacrifice when you do it for someone you love, is it?"

He flinched. Tears sparkled in his eyes. "Please, Lindsey."

She shook her head. "I'll explain your confession to the jury. We'll find more evidence. Evidence that exonerates you. I'll show the jury that you didn't kill your uncle, that you could never do such a thing. I'll hand them reasonable doubt on a silver platter." She waited, breathless. Wanting him to agree with her. Wanting desperately for things to be different.

"There is no evidence, Lindsey. No silver platter." Running his fingers through her hair, he pushed the stray tresses over her shoulder and smoothed his hand down her back. He leaned down and pressed his lips to the top of her head. "It's over, Lindsey. I want you to forget it and move on. For me."

She wrapped her arms around his waist and pressed her cheek against the hard muscle of his stomach. He felt so strong, so solid. She inhaled the essence that was his alone.

She couldn't forget. She couldn't move on. She didn't care about her career. She didn't care about her future. All she cared about was Bart, hearing him say her name…breathing in his clean, honest scent…loving him.

With all her heart, loving him.

Tears broke free, coursing down her cheeks. "You're wrong, Bart. It's not over. Not by a long shot. You said once that I never give up. Well, you were right. I don't give up. And I'm not going to give up on you."

He sucked in a sharp breath. "That's what I've always been afraid of."

Chapter Sixteen

Lindsey slumped in her office chair and tried not to look at the clock on her desk. The effort was wasted. She knew what time it was. She could feel every second tick by, drawing closer and closer to the scheduled time of Bart's allocution—the hearing where he would confess to three murders he didn't commit and receive his sentence. By agreeing to a plea bargain with the D.A., he had given up his right to a trial.

She'd worked so hard since she'd last seen him, spending countless hours overturning every stone she could in an effort to find evidence to clear him. But except for the report on the bottles and glass shards from Hit 'Em Again, she'd come up with nothing. And even the report had turned out to be negative for any kind of drug except alcohol.

The only thing she was left with was her faith. In Bart. In his goodness, his honesty. And in the court system. And stacked against Bart's confession, that didn't add up to much.

Or did it?

The last time she'd talked to Bart, she'd threatened

to go to the judge, to challenge Bart's confession, to tell him everything she knew, whether she could prove it or not. Bart had been right that a move like that wouldn't solve the problem. That the best they could hope for was for the judge to throw the question to a jury—a jury that would probably look no further than Bart's confession. It certainly wasn't the solution she was hoping for, but at least it would postpone his sentencing. At least it would buy some time.

Pushing back from her desk, she stood and strode out of her office and down the hall. Maybe she could catch Paul before he left for the courthouse, tell him her plan.

The door to Paul's office was open. A good sign. She rounded the bend and stepped inside.

Nancy Wilks stood at Paul's vacant desk. Her dark bob, usually harnessed rigidly in place by loads of hair spray, looked mussed. Her eyes darted to Lindsey, as if she'd been caught going through Paul's private papers. She held up a cigarette in shaking fingers and bobbed her head. "Lindsey?"

"I need to talk to Paul."

"He already left for court."

Lindsey's heart dropped.

Nancy gathered up a stack of files on Paul's desk. Taking a drag off her cigarette, she started for the door. "I'm heading to the courthouse in just a few minutes. If you want, I can pass on a message."

Lindsey hesitated. An uneasy feeling crept up her spine. There was something about Nancy's tone. Something wrong. As if she suspected Lindsey was hiding something? As if she was hiding something herself? "Thanks anyway, Nancy. I'll just give Paul a call on his cell phone. He has it with him, doesn't he?"

Nancy raised a controlled eyebrow. "Of course."

Lindsey stepped to the side of the desk and picked up the phone. Her hand trembled as she held the cordless receiver. She quickly tapped in Paul's number. The ring on the line sounded in her ear, blending with the buzz of nerves. "Thanks, Nancy."

Giving her one last look, Nancy turned and walked from the room, leaving a trail of cigarette smoke behind her.

After several rings with no answer, Lindsey replaced the phone in its cradle. Leaving a voice mail would do no good if he didn't get his messages until after the hearing. She needed to get down to the courthouse, and she needed to get there now. She stepped away from the desk, her foot plowing into the metal trash can.

It fell to its side. Blackened ash spilled over the money-green carpet.

Ash? Paul didn't smoke. Why would there be ash in his wastebasket? She leaned closer. She could make out two slips of paper. Reports of some kind. Lab reports. The name of the lab to which Doc Swenson had sent Bart's samples was legible at the top of each page.

She lowered herself to her knees and blew a stream of air at the reports to clear away some of the ash. The half-charred name at the top of both was Bart Rawlins. One address was the office and the other was her apartment. Two copies of the same report. One must have been stolen from her apartment in the break-in. Farther down, a number indicated the level of Rohypnol in Bart's system. And even though she was no scientist, she recognized the number as being high.

Very high.

Her pulse beat a frantic rhythm. She grabbed an envelope from the desk. Poking and prodding, she pushed the slips of paper into it, careful not to destroy any fingerprints there might be. Ash floated into the air around her. The rest of the reports were destroyed, but she'd seen all she needed to see. The report she'd received earlier was a fake.

And if she hadn't interrupted Nancy, she never would have found the originals.

LINDSEY RACED up the steps of the Mustang Valley Courthouse. She had to reach Bart. She had to show him and Paul what she'd found. She had to tell them what Nancy had done before it was too late.

When she'd driven out of the Lambert & Church parking lot, Nancy's car had still been parked in its usual space. Lindsey had beat her to the courthouse, but there wasn't a moment to spare. Bart's hearing was drawing near.

Heels clacking on marble, she negotiated the maze of hallways leading to Judge Valenzuela's courtroom. People bustled and gathered outside the courtroom. The doors were open and flanked by bailiffs, and inside Lindsey could see a crowd of reporters and citizens.

She turned a corner and headed for the lawyer-client meeting rooms to the side of the courtroom. Only one was occupied. She rapped on the door with a shaking hand.

Paul pulled it open and peered out. "Lindsey?"

"I have to talk to you and Bart."

"Now's not the time. We're due in court soon."

"It's urgent."

He frowned but stepped back to let her slip inside.

Bart pushed to his feet on the other side of a small table, watching her through sad and wary eyes. He looked thin and pale in his jail jumpsuit, more like his father than the robust cowboy she'd met at the beginning of this ordeal. The cowboy she'd fallen in love with.

Her heart pinched.

Paul closed the door. "This had better be worth it, Lindsey."

It was worth it, all right. She kept her attention on Bart. She couldn't have done otherwise if her life depended on it. "I found the reports, Bart. The *real* lab reports. The ones that show high levels of Rohypnol in your system. The other one was a fake."

Lines dug into his brow. "What are you talking about, Lindsey?"

"Evidence. I'm talking about evidence that proves you couldn't have killed Jeb Rawlins."

His jaw tensed. His face hardened. As if he didn't

believe what she was saying. Or he was afraid to let himself hope.

"It won't make the judge drop the charges immediately. But it will give us some ammunition to take to a trial. Strong ammunition. The kind that produces reasonable doubt." She drew a deep breath, forcing all her conviction into her voice. "You can't plead guilty. You have to help me fight this."

"Let me see those reports," Paul held out his hand.

Lindsey clutched the envelope. She didn't want to let it go, even to show Paul. She wanted to hand it directly to the judge. She couldn't take the chance that whatever evidence it carried would be contaminated. "We don't have time. I have to show this to Judge Valenzuela. Nancy will be here any minute."

"Nancy?" Bart echoed. "What does this have to do with Nancy?"

"I'll tell you later. Just promise me one thing. Promise me you won't plead guilty."

"Lindsey—"

"Trust me on this, Bart. If I'm wrong, you can plead later. Just promise me you won't plead guilty. Have faith in me."

A full minute seemed to tick by. His eyes drilled into her. A muscle along his jaw flexed and released. Finally he dragged in a ragged breath. "I promise."

Relief spiraled through her. Forcing herself to turn away, she strode for the door on shaking legs, gripping the envelope like a lifeline.

"Lindsey?" Bart said.

She turned back. A shiver rippled up her spine. "What?"

"I've always had faith in you."

Tears welled in her eyes. She blinked them away. She didn't have time for tears now. She had to reach the judge. She had to give him the slip of paper that could save Bart's life. She reached for the doorknob.

A hand slammed against the door, holding it shut. "You're not going anywhere, Lindsey." Paul's voice was rough, strange.

She turned around and stared into the snub-nosed barrel of a gun.

Chapter Seventeen

Bart's heart jumped to his throat. He stared at the little revolver, its barrel leveled on Lindsey. "What the hell are you doing, Paul?"

Paul looked at the gun in his hand, as if just recognizing it was there. Then, his expression hardening, he took his free hand off the door and shoved it toward Lindsey, palm up. "Give it to me."

Lindsey's eyes flared wide and then narrowed on Paul, like she'd gotten a bead on him and not the other way around. "One of these reports is addressed to me at my apartment. You broke into my apartment that night, Paul? You stole my briefcase? But it wasn't my briefcase you were after, was it? It was my mail."

Paul's expression didn't change. "Give me the report."

"You knew all along Bart didn't kill Jeb. He couldn't have. He had too much Rohypnol in his system. Rohypnol Gary Tuttle slipped into his beer at the bar." Lindsey lifted her chin and met her boss's eye. "Who killed Jeb, Paul? You?"

Paul didn't answer. But he didn't have to. Bart

could see the guilt etched in the lines of his face, hard as the callousness in his eyes.

"So it wasn't Kenny," Bart muttered. He couldn't quite believe his cousin was innocent, but the evidence was right in front of him, shoving a gun in Lindsey's face.

The gun. He had to get that gun away from Paul. But to do that, he needed to get around this damn table without Paul seeing him move. He focused on Lindsey, willing her to look at him, to know what he was thinking.

Her blue gaze flicked toward him. And then held. She set her chin and drew in a deep breath. Breaking eye contact, she focused on her boss. "Why did you do it, Paul?"

Paul glanced at him and then back to Lindsey.

"I can't imagine what would make you do something like that," she continued. "What's in it for you?"

Paul shook his head in disgust. "Isn't it obvious?"

Bart took a silent step.

Lindsey frowned, a tiny line appearing between graceful eyebrows. "Obvious? How?"

Paul shifted his focus to Bart. "It's all your damn fault."

"How is it Bart's fault?" Lindsey raised her voice, trying to draw Paul's attention.

It worked. Paul turned to her with a glower. "If Bart would have sold the Four Aces when I originally approached him with the Ranger deal, and if his damn ornery cuss of an uncle hadn't jacked up the price of his land beyond reason, none of this would have had to happen.''

"The land? You killed three people over land?'' Lindsey prodded.

"I didn't kill Beatrice. Gary did. She got in his way when he was taking the old man out on the range.''

Poor Beatrice. She'd only been doing her job, trying to take care of his daddy, keep him safe. And Gary. After all his daddy had done for Gary... Bart pushed away the sting of betrayal. None of it mattered. The only thing he could think about now was stopping Paul. And saving Lindsey. He took another step toward the corner of the table.

"So you and Gary did all this for what?'' Lindsey continued. "Money?''

"The Bar JR and the Four Aces are worth a lot. More than you know.'' Paul scowled at her. "Maybe money doesn't seem like much for a Wellington or the owner of the Four Aces or for Don Church and his family millions. But some of us weren't handed money and influence at birth. Some of us had to scrape and scratch for every penny.''

Bart shook his head. Despite the current success of the Four Aces, there had been plenty of lean times. He could understand the frustration Paul felt at not being raised with money, at having to see Don dressed to the nines in his designer suits every day while Paul had to claw to build his end of the partnership. And he could understand Gary's desperation to retire from ranching after suffering years of back pain. Maybe even his desire for a few luxuries. Still, none of it made a damn bit of sense. No amount of frustration or pain or envy could justify murder.

Lindsey glanced at him before zeroing in on Paul. "You *murdered* Jeb and Gary. And you would have let Bart take the lethal injection for it."

Paul's lips flattened, but there was no remorse in his eyes.

Lindsey shook her head. "I can't believe you almost got away with it."

"I did get away with it. Bart signed the papers. The ranches belong to Ranger now, and the cut of future profits Roger promised is mine."

"Not yet. Bart isn't convicted. He isn't going to plead. I saw Nancy in time."

"What the hell does Nancy have to do with this?" Paul asked.

"She didn't burn the lab report or help you cover up evidence?"

"You think she's in on this? Please. Nancy is a glorified bookkeeper. She doesn't have the imagination or the ambition."

"Then what was she doing in your office this morning?"

Paul's brow furrowed. "I don't have a clue. Probably snooping. I'll deal with her later."

"How about Brandy Carmichael?" Lindsey pressed on.

Paul flinched at the name. "She's just a mistake from my past."

"She told us about your affair. She also told us she

wanted to list Jeb's land. Was she after that deal with Ranger Corporation, too?''

Paul's brows shot toward his hairline. ''You think you have this all figured out, don't you? Did you also figure out why I gave you Bart's case when you had no experience in criminal law, let alone murder?''

Lindsey sucked in a breath.

''That's right. I thought you'd blow it. And you did.''

Bart clenched his teeth until his jaw hurt. Lindsey hadn't blown it. She'd saved him. Despite the way he'd played right into Paul's hands in a misguided attempt to protect her, she'd saved him. And he was damn well going to get the chance to thank her. He took another stealthy step.

Paul's eyes shifted, like he'd caught movement out of the corner of his eye.

Bart froze.

Lindsey reached for the door.

Paul grabbed her arm and jammed the muzzle of the gun into her ribs. ''What the hell do you think you're doing?''

Every nerve in Bart's body screamed for him to jump Paul, to get that damn gun. But the table still blocked him. And though he'd seen such heroics in movies, in real life the move would probably only get them killed. He forced himself to take only a small step, a step Paul wouldn't notice. He had to get into position before he made a move. It was Lindsey's only chance.

Lindsey glared into Paul's eyes, like the gun in her

ribs didn't even faze her. "We're in the courthouse, Paul. There are bailiffs just outside the door. You're not going to get away with this."

"That's where you're wrong. You and I are going to walk out this door and right under those bailiffs' noses. And you aren't going to try anything."

Bart's heart slammed against his ribs. Paul obviously didn't know Lindsey like he did. She would try something. He would bet his life on it. And Paul would shoot her. Fear clutched his throat. He couldn't let Paul take her out that door. He had to put an end to this now. He inched around the corner of the table.

"But how's that going to work?" Lindsey continued. "Bart will be here by himself. You really don't think he's just going to sit here politely while you're gone."

"That's exactly what he's going to do if he doesn't want me to put a bullet in you. And when I get back, he's going to go into that courtroom and plead guilty for killing Jeb, Gary and Beatrice. And he's going to make it convincing."

"How does he know you aren't going to put a bullet in me as soon as we step outside the courthouse?"

Paul smiled. "I guess he'll just have to have faith in me."

Not in this lifetime. Bart met Lindsey's eyes. He took the last step around the table.

Lindsey dropped to the floor.

Bart charged. Before Paul had time to swing the gun around, he drove into Paul's side like a linebacker.

Breath exploded from the attorney's lungs.

Bart plowed a fist into his jaw.

Paul raised his gun hand.

Bart chopped down on his arm. The gun clattered to the floor. He found the lawyer's face with another punch and another, until Paul lay still.

Grabbing the gun, Lindsey scrambled to her feet and rushed for the door. The noise of the crowds in the hall had probably prevented the bailiffs outside from hearing the fight, but Lindsey obviously intended to call them in now.

Bart caught her as her fingers touched the knob. "Wait."

She turned to him. Eyes bright and skin flushed that delicate pink, she looked as beautiful and strong as he'd ever seen her. She searched his eyes.

"Once you get the bailiffs in here, we won't be able to talk. And I have some things you need to hear."

She shook her head. "You have faith in me. You were willing to put your life on the line. You saved my life. That's all I need to know."

"Then there's something I need to say." He gathered her against him. She was so soft and yet strong. Ladylike yet as tenacious as his best cutting horse. "I love you, Lindsey."

Tears sparkled in her blue eyes. "I love you too, Bart. And I'll get you cleared. I promise."

He shook his head. "I only need one promise from you."

"Anything."

"Promise me that when this mess is over, you'll let me prove how much you mean to me."

"I promise, Bart. With all my heart, I promise."

Holding each other close, they moved toward the door as one.

Epilogue

"What are you going to do now, Lindsey?" Cara's concerned voice rippled over Lindsey's cell phone.

The million-dollar question. Lindsey threw her car into Park but didn't open the door. Instead she sat in the air-conditioning and watched lights glowing from the house, apartment building and interim horse barn at the Four Aces.

Her head was still spinning. It was impossible to wrap her mind around all that had gone on in the past few days since Paul had drawn a gun on her and Bart at the courthouse. So much had come to light. So much had changed. And now the news Cara had just given her. None of it seemed real.

"Lindsey? Are you there?"

Lindsey brought her mind back to her conversation. Cara had asked what she was going to do now. What *was* she going to do now? Don had offered to keep her on while he sorted out the wreckage of Lambert & Church, but she hadn't given him her answer. "Is this Cara the reporter asking?"

"No. Cara the friend."

She blew a breath of air through tight lips. "I'm sorry. I'm still trying to recover from the bombshell you just dropped on me."

"Don't worry about it. Being called a reporter in any context is no insult to me. You know that."

Yes, she did. Cara was a top-notch reporter through and through. And she and Kelly were top-notch friends.

"Are you still staying at the Four Aces?" Cara asked.

Lindsey looked out the windshield of her parked car. "Bart has been insisting I stay here until he's sure I'm no longer in danger. That protective thing he's got going."

"Yeah, and I'm sure that's all it is," Cara teased. "As long as he's protecting you in bed at night, that's all that matters."

"Cara!"

"Don't tell me you're still living a chaste life. I'll have to come out there and slap you."

No, there was nothing chaste about the life she'd been living at the Four Aces since the sheriff had found so much evidence of Paul's wrongdoing hidden at his house that the D.A. had been forced to drop the charges against Bart. Just thinking about the nights since Bart had been released from jail brought heat to her cheeks and a silly grin to her face. "There will be no slapping, Cara."

"Good girl. Now back to my original question. What are you going to do now?"

"Ranger Corporation is threatening to sue Bart for

backing out of the sale. I suppose I'll be busy working on that.''

''What about long-term, Lindsey?''

''Long-term? I guess I have some thinking to do.''

''Fair enough. I just don't want you deciding to move back to Boston.''

Move back to Boston? She hadn't thought of that option. Maybe because it wasn't one. ''Mustang Valley is my home. You're not getting rid of me that easily.''

''Glad to hear it,'' Cara said with certainty, as if all her questions were answered. A remarkable feat.

Too bad Lindsey's questions weren't answered. And sitting in her car chatting with Cara wasn't about to answer them, either. ''I have to go.''

After exchanging goodbyes, Lindsey punched the End button on her cell phone and climbed into the warm Texas night. She needed to find Bart. She needed to tell him what had happened. Maybe then she could put her life in order in her own mind. Maybe then she could answer some of the questions plaguing her.

She spotted him walking from the barn, a big palomino horse trailing behind him. Although the horse wore a bridle, his back was bare. As soon as Bart spotted her, a smile spread over his lips. ''Just the woman I'm looking for.'' He narrowed his eyes and studied her face. ''What happened?''

Cara's news. Shock must still be written all over her face. ''Cara called.''

''And?''

"The grand jury indicted Paul for both Jeb's and Gary's murders and for drugging and framing you."

"After all the evidence they found at his house and office, it's no wonder."

She nodded.

"So if Cara called just to tell you that, why the long face?"

"That's not all she told me." She took a deep breath. "They found Paul in his jail cell after the news of the indictment came down. He hanged himself."

Bart's lips tightened. "I can't say I'm too sorry about that."

"Me, either, I guess. It's just that the whole thing is so sad. I took the position at Lambert & Church because Paul seemed to believe in me. He made me think I could be a success."

"You are a success, Lindsey. You don't need Paul. You don't need Lambert & Church. You don't need anybody."

"That's not true. I need you. But not to believe I'm a success. I just need you to be happy."

"Damn straight. And İ need you, too." He stepped forward and gathered her into his arms.

Warmth seeped into her bones and wrapped around her heart. She drew in a deep breath of leather and fresh air. He was something, her cowboy. Honest and tender and strong all wrapped into one sexy package.

He pulled back slightly and looked down at her. Mischief twinkled in her green eyes. "All this brings me to the reason for this horse." He raised the rein he held in one hand and the palomino stepped forward.

She gave Bart a questioning look.

"The other night I wished I could take you for a moonlight ride. Tonight I aim to make that wish come true."

Anticipation shivered through her. The thought of snuggling close to Bart while a horse's back rocked gently beneath them was more tempting than chocolate. "I'll go change into jeans."

"Don't bother. I don't envision us needing a lot of clothing for this ride."

Another shiver sent heat to her core.

"But before we go riding, I have a question to ask."

"A question?"

"Yes. And I want an honest answer, so help you God."

As if she could meet Bart's sincerity with anything less. She raised her right hand. "So help me, God."

Dropping the rein, effectively ground-tying the horse, Bart fitted a large palm over his hat and lifted it off his head. "After that ordeal with Paul in the courthouse, I said I only wanted one promise."

She remembered. How could she forget? "You said you wanted me to let you prove how much you loved me."

"Yes. But I've decided that isn't enough."

She willed him to go on, to tell her what more he wanted, what more she would gladly give.

Holding his hat to his heart with one hand and taking Lindsey's hand in the other, he sank to one knee. "When I met you, I'd all but given up on finding a woman I wanted to spend forever with. But I found that with you. I don't know what the future is going to bring, but I do know I want to spend it with you. I want you to be my bride.''

Joy spun through her, making her giddy.

"I know you want to build your career, and I'm fine with that. I've been a bachelor so long I can take care of myself and Daddy and you. We can do this, Lindsey. You won't have to sacrifice a thing."

"Oh, Bart. You don't have to convince me. I would be honored to be your bride. I would be honored to spend the rest of my days loving you." She reached down and smoothed her fingertips over his stubbled chin. Decisions fell into place in her mind, decisions she hadn't known she'd made until this moment. "I want to set up a practice to help people who can't help themselves. Children. And people like your father."

He nodded, pride spreading over his face in a wide grin.

"And after I establish my new law practice, I want children of our own. I want to fill all the bedrooms in that big house of yours."

He pushed to his feet. Fitting his hat back on his head, he wrapped his arms around her. "You've just made me the happiest man in Texas, maybe the whole damn country. We can get the marriage license and rings tomorrow and be married by next week."

She pulled back from his embrace. "We have to wait for your father to get out of the rehabilitation center. He has to be at the wedding."

Bart's brow furrowed briefly as if considering this

new wrinkle. He nodded. "He's doing better every day, so that shouldn't be too long."

"And we have to wait until my family can come to the wedding."

He looked at her out of the corner of his eye. "Of course."

"And Cara and Kelly. We have to wait for Kelly to get back from her honeymoon."

"Okay. Is that all?"

"It would be nice if you and Kenny could reconcile."

His grimace broke into a smile. "Well, I guess I can try. It's not sacrifice if you do it for someone you love."

Joy spread over her lips and burst in her soul like Fourth of July fireworks. Kenny aside, the thought of a wedding to the man of her dreams witnessed by all the people she loved filled her nearly to bursting.

He chuckled and folded her back into his arms.

She reveled in the feel of him, so strong, so solid, so warm. It didn't matter what the future brought. As long as she had Bart, she could weather anything. As long as she had Bart, every day for the rest of her life would be a stunning success.

*Turn the page for a sneak
preview of the next gripping*

SHOTGUN SALLYS *title,*
LAWFUL ENGAGEMENT

*by popular author Linda O. Johnston
on sale in July 2004
in Harlequin Intrigue...*

Chapter One

Cara Hamilton's heart beat a familiar, thunderous tattoo of anticipation deep inside her chest. She parked at the curb, slung her large purse over her shoulder and exited her small Toyota.

It was nearly one o'clock in the morning. Though most residences along Caddo Street were dark, lights blazed in the first-floor apartment of the three-story converted Victorian in front of her. Cara's friend Nancy Wilks, who lived there, had called half an hour ago. She hadn't said much, only that she had something important to show Cara.

But Cara sensed that, whatever it was, it could be the key to the biggest story in her life.

That was why she felt the familiar rush of excitement. She was on the trail of something newsworthy. And this time it was something *beyond* newsworthy. Something that could blow the blasé citizens of Mustang Valley right out of their couch-potato seats. Make her career.

Only…as she stood outside her car and glanced around the sleeping neighbourhood, a sudden, strange chill enveloped Cara. It was northeast Texas in midsummer. Humid and warm, even at night. Too hot to make her feel so cold.

As she shivered nonetheless, her skin prickled.

"It's the news itch," she whispered aloud, determined to shrug off her inexplicable uneasiness. "I've been stung by the tattle bug. Right, Sally?"

As if her idol Shotgun Sally, the stuff of incredibly inspirational folklore, could respond. But as usual, the silly little device of talking to her, using her legendary language, lifted Cara's spirits.

Not that she'd do so where anyone else could hear.

Cara flinched at the click of her car door closing. The night had been silent except for the crisp chirping of crickets, and their singing halted at the sound. Not even traffic noise from the highway, only a few miles away. And nothing at all from the direction of downtown Mustang Valley.

Cara's own deep and uneven breathing broke the stillness. That and the light tap of her boot heels on the pavement.

The humidity hung heavy in the air, stifling Cara, moistening her bare arms, for she wore a short-sleeved blouse tucked into her long skirt that matched the soft buckskin-colored vest over it. Why didn't the heavens just split into a thunderstorm and get it over with?

She winced as her footsteps grew louder when she walked up the three steps to the wooden porch. So what? She was expected.

"Nancy? Where are you?"

If Cara had felt unnerved before, now she trembled

with tension. Tattle bug? Heck, she felt as if an army of ants marched formations along her spine.

"Nancy?" Cara called. She glanced into the living room. Though the lamps on either side of the floral print sofa were lit, the room was empty. She continued down the hall.

The farthest door on the right, the one to the bedroom, was ajar. "Nancy?" Cara's voice rasped, and she cleared her throat. No reason to feel so weird. Nancy was probably in the bathroom with the door closed, the water running so she couldn't hear Cara.

But neither could Cara hear water in the pipes.

She called out once more, "Nancy," as she pushed the bedroom door open. And gasped.

Nancy was there. Wearing a pink top and blue jeans, she lay on her bed, facedown, her dark hair askew as her head hung over the side.

"What's wrong?" Cara cried as she dashed over to her friend, who remained motionless.

Cara's question was answered in less than a moment, when she turned Nancy over. Her eyes were closed—and there was an ugly, black-rimmed red hole in the middle of her forehead. And so much blood...

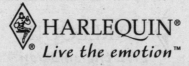

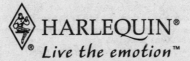

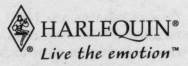